The Celaran Pact
(Book 10 of the PIT Series)
by Michael McCloskey
Copyright 2017 Michael McCloskey
ISBN: 978-1981101863

Learn more about Michael McCloskey's works at
www.squidlord.com

Cover art by Stephan Martiniere
Edited by Stephen 'Shoe' Shoemaker

Chapter 1

The might of the combined Terran-Celaran fleet assembled a light minute from Celara Palnod for an offensive campaign against their shared enemy, the Quarus. Telisa monitored the formations in her PV as she waited for Admiral Sager to appear incarnate. The fleet would deploy as a planar screen of robotic ships with partitioned Terran or Celaran flotillas behind it. The flotillas were uniformly either Terran or Celaran because the allies each had their own strengths and weaknesses. Keeping the flotillas limited to a single type allowed each flotilla to operate tightly together, with similar engagement closing velocities and tactics. Each flotilla was composed of six (Celaran) or ten (Terran) squadrons of three to seven ships whose combined firepower was deemed sufficient to destroy one enemy ship at a time.

The entire fleet could close into a spherical formation if necessary, but the plan was to engage with most units at the front to ensure the majority of the fleet could simultaneously fire at optimal ranges. It was standard Space Fleet doctrine—if only part of your fleet could shoot at the enemy at any given time, then you were wasting the rest of your firepower.

Telisa's enhanced hearing told her of Admiral Sager's arrival before the door opened. She shifted in her seat to greet him.

"Admiral," she nodded without rising from her bridge lounge.

"Team Member," he said. He forwent the salute, knowing she did not favor that protocol.

"You said you have something for me?"

"Some people from Sol want to help you," Sager said, seating himself. "I'm hoping you'll hear out their offers FTF."

"I appreciate that you want to help us grow our numbers, and that's on my list, but do we really have time for face to face? There must be a thousand incomalcons who want to join the PIT team."

"If I may disagree, Team Member," Sager said carefully. He paused for just the right amount of time as if waiting for approval, yet charged on a bit too fast for Telisa to actually offer it. "I've vetted these heavily from a pool of almost one million applicants. I've screened the crowd down to only two people that had something important enough to offer that they're here now."

"A million? A million applicants?" Telisa asked, aghast.

"*Almost* one million, yes. I've cut it down to two. They've traveled here from Sol to meet with you."

From a million applicants, down to two! He knows I won't refuse after hearing that.

"Magnus, please come to the bridge immediately," Telisa sent.

She had told Magnus that she would not need him for the meeting, for which he gladly thanked her. But now...

"Give me a minute," he replied. He sounded more intrigued than irritated.

While Telisa waited, she considered the situation. Her first thoughts leaned toward paranoia. Would Shiny have been able to get someone this far through cleverness and subterfuge? Or straight out mind control?

Magnus hurried into the room. He wore a glossy new Veer suit over his solid frame. He had configured it to black and red by habit.

"Admiral," he said to Sager.

"Glad to have you join us, TM. Did Team Member Telisa fill you in?"

Magnus shook his head.

"I have two very special—critical, in my opinion—candidates for you to interview for the effort against the Quarus."

"For the PIT team?" Magnus asked.

"Not necessarily," Sager said.

"These two were culled from almost a million," Telisa added. Magnus looked suitably impressed. He sat down.

"Bring the first one in," Telisa said.

"Stracey Stalos of Guriti Nervous Integration," a synthetic voice announced.

An attractive woman of indeterminate age walked in. Telisa and Magnus rose to greet her. Stracey Stalos had large eyes and shiny black hair. In many ways, she looked like Telisa—slender and the same height with matching hair—but Ms. Stalos had an air of delicate elegance rather than Telisa's stout, rugged athleticism.

I know this person somehow, don't I? But her face isn't familiar, only her name.

"I'm very happy to be here," Stracey said. "It's an honor to meet more Team Members."

More team members? Nope. I still don't know who this is.

Stracey flashed a smile. "No need to introduce yourselves, of course. I know you're Telisa and you're Magnus," she said, looking at each of them in turn. "I'm Stracey and I head GNI."

They each held their hands forward, slightly slanted in the Core Worlder touchless greeting. Telisa sat back down and Stracey sat a second later.

"What have you come all this way for?" Telisa said directly. Her voice sounded a bit hard to her own ears.

"GNI has been working on a project to protect host bodies from Trilisk control," Stracey said. "I've been directly involved since the beginning, as it's something of a pet project for me. I'd like to perfect our approach with the PIT team, if you'll work with me, and offer you any solution we can forge."

Telisa bristled and her alertness heightened.

"Really? How did you learn about host bodies, dare I ask?"

"After TM Yang discussed it with me, Ambassador Shiny was kind enough to provide us with data about the host bodies. He's also eager to solve this problem."

Jason Yang! Okay, that mystery is solved.

"Honestly, I'm surprised Shiny would share that kind of information with you. Still, have you cracked the problem?"

"We believe we're very close. I tried to contact TM Yang, but with him so far out on-mission, I haven't been able to get word to him. The Space Force interviewed me and offered me transport here once I explained what GNI has to offer."

"That's amazing. The PIT team would like to review what you've learned."

"I hope to administer the treatment on you," Stracey said. "If you're dealing with Trilisks, it could save you."

"I haven't told her the nature of our current mission," Admiral Sager sent to Telisa and Magnus privately.

"Come with me to our Vovokan support ship later," Telisa said. "I'd like you to meet our xenobiologist and explain what you've developed to him."

"I'm not sure it can be... *grasped* that easily," Stracey said. "It took a team of—"

"My person can grasp it," Telisa said, purposefully using the same word Stracey had chosen.

"Of course," she said. Telisa supposed she knew better than to argue with a TM.

How did I get so powerful?

"Once our TM approves, we can put together a plan for collaboration. How long do you think it would take to create a prototype from your research?"

"I think we could accomplish it in a couple months, maybe faster."

Not enough time to take care of it before the campaign. Telisa did not reveal her disappointment at that timeline. *Besides, I don't trust this woman or her corporation.*

"Is TM Yang available?" Stracey asked. "Maybe I could say hi while I'm waiting for you to finish here?"

Telisa took a deep breath.

"If we tell too many people about the copies it'll get out fast," Magnus shot in privately.

"Exactly what I was worried about," Telisa replied electronically. "Though she knows about the host bodies already. I wonder if GNI has kept that secret. They may well have, for their own potential benefit."

"I'm sorry, but Jason isn't here," Telisa said to Stracey.

"Of course. You all have very important work to do."

"Please wait just a while longer, and I'll escort you to our research vessel," Telisa said.

Research vessel. Right. But she'll be impressed by the Vovokan hardware. I wonder if Maxsym and her will hit it off?

"Thank you for this opportunity," Stracey said. After a heartbeat, she stood.

Telisa felt awkward for not standing, so instead she said, "It won't be long."

Stracey nodded and walked out.

"Well, I can see why she made the cut," Telisa said to Sager. "If GNI is serious about fixing this vulnerability, that could be a huge advance for us."

"My thoughts exactly."

"Well we know why Shiny wants to 'solve this problem'," Magnus said. "He wants to control the host bodies directly the same way Trilisks do."

"I suppose... but he already controls us, more or less," Telisa said.

She paused, but Admiral Sager did not comment.

Telisa continued.

"Okay, I'm warming up to this. Too bad we're already half done. Send in the next."

Sager nodded.

"Aiye of Core World Security," the synthetic voice announced. The door opened.

That voice is making me feel like a queen being visited by subjects.

A humanoid machine advanced through the doorway, wearing a Space Force uniform with the rank of Colonel. The android had silvery skin and a green circle on its uniform, clearly marking it as artificial. The android had only a smooth sensor plate for a face, curved to fit the shape of its head. It held a small black case by a handle.

"I am Aiye," it said, declining its head slightly.

"Nice to meet you," Telisa said. She worked at being more polite now that she had wrapped her head around how important this meeting could be. "What do you do, Aiye?"

"I oversee monitoring the Sol system to detect Trilisk invaders," Aiye said.

Telisa raised an eyebrow.

Important, indeed.

"Then it's an honor to meet you," Telisa said. "You've strayed a long way from Sol."

"Admiral Sager has allowed me to come here and offer my assistance to this fleet," Aiye explained. "The technology and protocols I deployed remain in place at Sol and are being monitored by my second."

Telisa nodded.

"How is the monitoring accomplished?"

The android opened the small case it had carried in and brought out a matte black sphere with a fractal pattern of ridges etched across its surface. It was half again larger than Telisa's attendant spheres wandering nearby.

"I carefully studied the devices which TM Yang used to find Trilisks on Earth," Aiye explained. "Once their principles of operation were understood, I created this mobile design that is even more sensitive."

"And you deployed these in the Solar System?"

"Yes."

"So were there Trilisks present?"

"Yes and no. Three places did trigger the signals, but we have not been able to—"

Telisa moved forward in her seat and almost stood.

"Which three places?"

"One on Earth. An island in the Mediterranean Sea..."

Telisa relaxed a notch.

"Ah. Yes. Go on."

Aiye's tilted its head as if puzzled, but it continued.

"Two locations in the outer system," Aiye said. It waited to see if Telisa would dismiss that information as well.

"The outer system, hrm. Impressive detection abilities! So let me guess, Shiny told you that your devices were working but that there was nothing to worry about."

Aiye nodded. "You're absolutely right, TM Relachik. Ambassador Shiny said that it was not a malfunction. He said that we had detected active Trilisk *technologies* in use, but that they were under his control."

Telisa steepled her hands.

Probably the AIs. Unless he somehow trapped a Trilisk in his columns and did not blow them up as he told us he would? Or if Shiny is controlled by a Trilisk, it might have chosen to stay hidden. But Shiny's actions don't seem like those of a Trilisk... once again, it could be concealing its plan.

"Returning to the island. Did you investigate that site?"

"There was already an active Vovokan installation there, and ambassador Shiny classified that place the same way."

"Very impressive, Aiye."

"So you knew about these, at least about the island?" Aiye asked.

"A man on my team discovered the island. There's a Trilisk compound there, so it makes sense it would be giving off these clues even if Trilisks are no longer present. I have good theories about the other spots. Shiny has ships cloaked there, and I can verify that he uses powerful Trilisk devices."

Aiye nodded. "Interesting."

"Tell me more about the sensors."

"These devices are compact and fast. Hard to detect. If you need to find Trilisks within a star system, then this is the solution."

"Did you bring more?"

"I brought a hundred of them with me."

Telisa stared at the device before her.

This is great. Though detecting them is only part of the battle.

"Each module is only fifty percent more massive than your attendants here," Aiye added.

"I think we could use your help, Aiye. I have to discuss it with some other TMs, though," Telisa said. "Thank you for coming all the way out here."

Aiye nodded. "The universe is stimulating and complex. I'm glad to see more of it."

The android put its hardware back into the case and walked out.

"This is all wonderful. Sometimes I forget the PIT team is not an island. We have allies back home."

"I have more help to offer, this time directly from the Space Force," Sager said.

"We're in the middle of a huge Space Force fleet. I think you're already pulling your share," Telisa noted.

"Nevertheless. I know the Cylerans excel at close quarters combat, and you have the Vovokan battle spheres. Still, I wanted you to know that our own special forces are available."

Telisa opened her mouth to reply, envisioning first Terran marines, then combat robots... until she remembered something Cilreth had told her.

"An Avatar battle system?" she asked.

Sager blinked. "You're remarkably well informed, TM."

Telisa just smiled, so Sager continued.

"The Avatar Class Battle Module at your disposal is designated 'ACBM Mamba'."

"Thank you, Admiral. That will come in handy."

Sager nodded and shifted in his seat. He looked worried.

"Something else?" she asked.

"I don't think this ship would be best for the TMs in a fleet engagement," Sager said. "I would recommend moving to a more formidable ship."

"I suppose you have a point," Telisa said slowly.

"I've made a high energy weapons ship available for you," Sager said. "I'd urge you to move there."

"We have some..." Telisa struggled to find the appropriate words. "Sensitive research going on here that won't exactly work with a Space Force crew roaming around..."

"It's a new robotic vessel. There would only be one crew member, an engineer, assigned to the ship and I've vetted her extensively," Sager assured. "It's the largest class of automated ship we have."

"You've been doing a lot of vetting recently."

"One of the joys of being an admiral," Sager said.

Telisa understood the sentiment. As a leader, one faced endless decisions all day long. Telisa was lucky enough to still see the field—a privilege that she would lose if they ever hired a full ship's complement for the PIT team.

"Tell me about the engineer," she said.

Telisa received a pointer from Sager. She saw a Space Force personnel file at the other end.

"Lieutenant Sisela Barrai, an officer decorated for saving lives in Sol's asteroid belt when Shiny took over. She's intelligent, loyal, and a great fighter."

Sager stressed the last point heavily.

"A great fighter? But she's an engineer, right? I know the two aren't mutually exclusive, but why are you selling it so hard?"

"I think it would be a culture fit. The PIT team does as much combat training as Space Force marines, at least, when you're not on-planet. Then you do the real thing. Barrai has won several medals for both her virtual and incarnate combat prowess."

"Okay. But she's not up for the team, really, she's just on our ship."

Sager shrugged. "Then as a practical matter, she's part of your team, even if she stays Space Force and doesn't get the exalted rank."

"Fair enough."

Chapter 2

Siobhan stepped off the shuttle into the bay of the *Sharplight*, a robotic HEW cruiser. The bay was white and spotless, with seams of all shapes and sizes on the walls where various support equipment would fold out as-needed. Only one of the panels lay open, the niche of a loading robot which was offloading containers from the shuttle.

Telisa walked off the shuttle and paused next to her.

"So, we're not going to name it *Iridar*?" Siobhan asked half-seriously.

"We've already got two of them."

"This ship has some slickblack automated features that I'm interested in studying," Siobhan said. She had already spotted another row of cargo bay robots lined up against the far wall and was busy predicting their functions based on their various shapes and sizes.

Caden disembarked energetically behind them. Marcant plodded out after him.

"Where's Maxsym?" asked Caden.

"He wants to stay on the Vovokan ship. I think he's been relying on its computing power for his work," Telisa said. "He's being joined by Stracey Stalos of GNI. They're going to collaborate on a project to protect host bodies from Trilisk control."

"That's great," Siobhan said. "But what's the head of GNI going to have in common with him?"

"She's a truly gifted individual," Telisa said. "She's still active in research, apparently. She claims that the host body study is her pet project at the company."

"Maxsym will tell us if it's true," Caden said. "If she's a faker, he'll know it in sixty seconds."

"I'm happy she's over there," Telisa said. "One less person to keep from our secrets over here."

11

Lee darted out of the shuttle and flew a rapid circuit of the bay. She had about 100 meters to fly straight across, and perhaps half that to make a wide turn before dashing back.

She has to like that. More room to glide around, thought Siobhan.

"Speaking of people we hide secrets from, I think that's our Space Force engineer," Marcant said.

Siobhan looked over to the main ship's entrance to the bay. A dark-skinned woman in a Space Force uniform awaited them at a major bulkhead door. She looked strong. Her hair was buzzed short on the sides with a section of rowdy curls down the middle.

Telisa and Siobhan walked over to her while Caden and Marcant wandered around the bay. Magnus was supposed to bring another shuttle over with the AI in a few minutes.

"Welcome aboard the *Sharplight*, TM," the lieutenant snapped, coming to attention.

"Thank you. Are you the... I'm sorry, I don't know your title," Telisa said.

"Lieutenant Barrai of the *Sharplight*, TM," boomed the woman. "I serve as the ship's automated engineering officer."

"Thank you, Lieutenant. And you know who we are?"

"Yes, ma'am."

"Preliminary orders: Decks 10, 11, and 12 are off limits. TMs only. The same for the aft cargo bays. I'll update the ships' map to reflect that within the hour," Telisa said.

"Aye, ma'am," Barrai said.

"Any anomalies are to be reported to the PIT team immediately," Telisa continued.

"Aye, ma'am."

"The only people allowed on this ship are yourself, the TMs, and Admiral Sager. Only TMs can add to that list. If

Ambassador Shiny himself shows up at the airlock I want you to turn him away, is that clear?"

"Aye, ma'am."

"By the way, that wasn't an exaggerated example. If Shiny *does* show up don't let him in without our say so. Once we're settled, I'll arrange a meeting and we can discuss details. Do you have any questions?"

"Yes, ma'am. I can't tell Celarans apart. I heard there is one on your team—"

Barrai's eyes grew wide as Lee soared over in a flash. The lieutenant took a step back as Lee charged. Siobhan understood the reaction, because the Celarans always flew right up to everyone at alarming speed.

"Sorry, her arrival can be a bit overwhelming," Telisa said. "Lee has a link interface. It's Celaran, of course, but since we've taught our devices to interact, she has a unique identifier that our protocols understand. You can tell her by her link."

"Understood, ma'am."

"Lee, this is Lieutenant Barrai. She watches over the robots on this ship."

"Hello," Lee said over the channel. She flashed bright colors at the same time, saying the same thing on her skin. "Thank you for having us on your vine."

"Glad to meet you, TM," Barrai said, holding her composure. "It's not my ship, my *vine*, though, it belongs to the PIT team. It's my job to watch over the automated systems."

"Do any of the robots fly on bright days?" Lee asked, looping in the air. "We could have some fun!"

"A couple do, yes," Barrai said. "Some of the equipment spaces are small, so we have light maintenance flyers that can make their way through there."

"Oh, good!" Lee said.

"Any other questions?" Telisa asked.

"Yes, ma'am. Is it true that TMs are masters of hand-to-hand combat?"

What kind of question is that? thought Siobhan.

"To varying degrees," Telisa said dryly. "You don't have to call us TMs."

"Aye, ma'am. This lieutenant would be honored to train with you, ma'am. It's been VR only for over a month."

Desperate for training partners.

"Ah, I see. No one to train with incarnate here. Well, if you want to fight me, you'll have to earn it, Lieutenant," Telisa said. "Start with Maxsym or Marcant. You'll have to work your way up from there."

New one on me.

"Aye, ma'am!"

"I'm sure they'll be in the ship's directory for non-urgent messages by the end of the day. Dismissed."

Lieutenant Barrai hurried away.

Telisa almost never dismisses anyone like that. But I guess we needed to clear her out for the arrival of the AI.

Telisa turned to Siobhan.

"She's an outstanding hand-to-hand fighter. She's won a slew of medals fighting in Space Force competitions. It's one small reason Sager chose her for our ship. He probably encouraged her to ask that."

"Maxsym or Marcant?" Siobhan asked innocently.

Telisa smiled.

"They need the practice."

Some humility might do Marcant some good, Siobhan thought. *Though neither of them has ever been physically overbearing.*

"It's not exactly fair to sic her on them," Siobhan said mildly.

"It's not about any kind of petty revenge," Telisa said. "Their skills will benefit from fighting her, and she'll get her chance to interact with the team. If she fights me right off, then I'd either have to hold back or explain the host body situation."

Siobhan nodded.

Caden came back over to Siobhan after his brief tour of the bay.

"Let's go to our deck and see what it's like," Caden said.

The Terrans walked over to the main dock corridor which led deeper into the ship. The map service told Siobhan they would take a vertical tube up from the corridor to the deck that housed the team. As they navigated the corridor, Siobhan explored the other services available. Most of them—maps, drinks, clothing, and so forth—were so common she barely noticed them. A few stood out as new.

"Got anything you want fried to a crisp? I have access to ship's weapons," Siobhan said.

"Me too!" Caden said.

"Five Holy Entities," Telisa said, rolling her eyes. "The kids can fire the high-energy weapons."

Siobhan knew Telisa was kidding. They went into combat with half a dozen deadly weapons all the time. Telisa trusted them with her life.

"We wouldn't shoot anything except in an emergency," Caden protested.

"Fine. Don't start another interstellar war. One is one too many," Telisa said.

They climbed into a tube and let a flow of air move them up through a gravity-free zone. Caden grabbed Siobhan's leg from below and pulled himself next to her. They grinned at each other like a couple of idiots.

Telisa stepped out of the tube. Caden and Siobhan followed her, stepping out as one. According to the map, their quarters were only tens of meters away.

"See you in a few?" Caden asked, winking.

Siobhan smiled back. "'Lutely!"

She walked to her door and noted Caden was housed close nearby. It recognized her and opened, revealing a large octagonal room with three other doorways.

"What?" Siobhan said stupidly. She had expected a one-room living space, but this looked more like the common room of a dormitory.

"Call me King Lonrack!" Caden said to her over their personal channel.

"I know, right? It's almost as nice as the *Clacker* was."

"Hey, and we have an AI! This place will be amazing."

Siobhan did not know if Telisa would allow them to use the Trilisk device so frivolously. A quick check of the three rooms that adjoined the central one made Siobhan suspect that this design had been derived from a shared living space for three regular crew members.

This is a robotic ship, so this deck must have been adapted from other designs in the fleet.

Suddenly a link connection came through from Shiny. *Shiny!*

She accepted the connection.

"TM Siobhan listens, Shiny delineates, explains, provides requirements."

"What? I—it's just you and me on the channel?"

"Correct. Shiny requires secret, obfuscated, hidden repayment, return, reciprocation of previous favor."

A feeling of suffocating dread dropped over Siobhan as she parsed his statement.

Of course this would happen.

"You need me to repay you for the help you gave me in overcoming Spero."

"Correct."

I didn't care about anything past getting my revenge. Now Shiny's ready to call it in.

"You helped me. So I'll help you..." She was afraid to breathe.

Suddenly, Caden signaled at her door service. She had not yet configured it to let him in.

"Wait a sec while I get it set up, okay?" she sent him.

"What do I do?" she asked Shiny.

"Siobhan prevents, stops, averts peaceful resolution of conflict between Celaran-Terran fleet and Quarus."

Purple. Pasted. Packets.

"How long could it take?" Caden asked from outside her door.

"Prevent peaceful... You want *me* to keep them from ending the war? How could I do that?"

"Siobhan resourceful, clever, scheming. Await chances, opportunities, openings. Others must not know of Siobhan objective, goal, purpose. Target Quarus system planets must be destroyed. Siobhan honors agreement with Shiny."

"I'll try, but—"

"Siobhan honors agreement with Shiny or else cooperative mode with Siobhan is shown to be without value, worth, profit."

Leaving only competitive mode.

"Look, if this is a bad time, just say so," Caden told her.

"Understood," Siobhan forced the answer out. The connection with Shiny dropped.

Destroy that system or no more Mr. Nice Shiny.

"Siobhan?"

"I'm... just busy setting everything up," she said to Caden. "Come on in."

Siobhan tried her best to smile normally when he walked in.

"Tell me what's up," he said, looking at her carefully.

"Stuff I want to forget about," she dodged. "Let's get some VR time."

Michael McCloskey

Chapter 3

"Intruder alert!"

Magnus's link awakened him swiftly with the emergency message. He checked his context in the darkness: he was in his own quarters halfway through third shift.

He felt Telisa moving, sliding out of the sleep web they shared. Magnus rolled out after her, slightly off kilter. Telisa caught him with supernatural balance and strength, righting him.

Magnus told the lights in his quarters to activate with a thought. Telisa was already halfway into her Veer suit.

"Vault room! By the Five, the AI!!!" she almost wailed.

Magnus put his legs into his Veer suit in record time. He grabbed the breaker claw and a laser pistol he had left lying around his room. He rejected the idea of taking his rifle for use on the ship.

Telisa bolted from the room, not even fully into her suit yet. Magnus had a split second image of Caden or Marcant getting an eyeful of their leader half hanging out of her Momma Veer. Then he was running after her.

"Hold on!" he sent on the team channel. "This is not a drill. We go in there together."

He sent a location pointer indicating the last hallway before the bridge that connected through to the vault room. The vault room was shown on the map adjacent to the main arsenal. The massive structure of the vault room protected the arsenal and the bridge from attacks coming in through the forward firing arc.

"It could be an ambush," said Caden. "I suggest Siobhan and I take the starboard entrance instead."

"Yes," Telisa said. "Marcant, seal off the vertical tubes going through the center of the ship. Adair, order Lieutenant Barrai to shelter in her quarters. She's not

19

allowed on that deck, but we have no idea where this might spill out."

"Done," Adair said.

"I'm sending the battle spheres here and here," Adair said, marking two spots on the map. The locations were on corridors heading toward the bow of the vessel, blocking two possible routes of escape from the vault room.

Magnus stopped thinking about tactics for a moment and asked the obvious question.

"How did they get into the vault room without being detected?"

"Team: Trilisk signs detected! Vault room!" Marcant rattled off.

Trilisk, that's how. A Trilisk has come for the AI!

"No!" Telisa yelled. The frustration must have been almost unbearable for her. For the first time in memory, she cursed aloud.

"I'm headed back," she told the team. "I'll go all the way aft. Magnus is in charge."

She turned back without another word. Her two attendants joined Magnus's, leaving him with four of the Vovokan spheres orbiting nearby.

Magnus studied the tactical as he ran to the last corridor. The bridge of the ship had three major entrances and exits to port, starboard, and aft, as well as a tube in the corner leading up and down. Marcant had approached the port entrance. If the vertical tubes were locked down, then they had the bridge surrounded. Magnus cycled through a hundred video feeds. He saw views from the other PIT members, their attendants, and the ship's internal sensors.

Arakaki awaited him at the aft bridge entrance in a combat suit with her submachine gun leveled. Two attendants orbited her.

Magnus found a video feed of the short walkway connecting the vault room with the arsenal. A large sapphire robot with three arms and three legs stood before the entrance to the vault room.

"It's a robot or a cyborg, in the arsenal walkway just off the bridge," Magnus announced. "I don't see any other enemies, but we're blind in the vault and the arsenal." He sent a pointer to the video feed to bring it to everyone's attention.

"That same kind of robot tricked me with video feeds before," Arakaki said. "Made me think it was somewhere it wasn't."

"I'm sending two attendants in," Magnus said.

The approach to the aft bridge door had no cover; he supposed that might be by design. The bridge had a laser emplacement on the ceiling with a 360-degree field of fire.

"Marcant, any signs of tampering? Do you think the laser on the bridge is still ours?"

"It appears to be under our control," Marcant said. His words told Magnus the truth: *with Trilisks, you could never be sure.*

On paper, the situation looked fine: they had the intruder "surrounded". In reality, the intruder could be a machine or a cyborg so advanced that it might be able to wink them all out of existence in a nanosecond. It might not even really be on the ship. Hell, *his team* might not even be on the ship.

That way madness lies. But what are we going to do? What CAN we do?

"Everyone hold," Magnus said. It grated to say it, but what would charging in on a robot that advanced accomplish other than their deaths? Perhaps the Vovokan battle spheres...

He watched the machine. It sat motionless. Was it waiting for them? Was it guarding the entrance while something happened beyond? The vault room and the arsenal had no sensor feeds. The PIT team had removed them to help ensure the Trilisk AI remained a secret.

"We can't take that thing out, not if it's really Trilisk," Magnus said. "Ideas anyone?"

"Alert the fleet," Caden said. "We'll abandon the *Sharplight* and let our capital ships reduce this cruiser to its component atoms."

"But what about the AI?" Magnus asked.

"Is the AI even still in there?" Marcant asked. "I don't see it on any of the feeds."

"Try to pray it away," Arakaki said.

"Would the AI really listen to us over it?"

"Depends on if it's a machine or a Trilisk cyborg, maybe," Caden said.

"I've dealt with this machine before," Telisa said. "It didn't harm me and I don't think it's controlled by a Trilisk mind."

Magnus checked her position. She had made it to the aft of the ship.

"So we should just send you in there to say hi?" Siobhan asked.

Arakaki turned to Magnus and spoke to him off-channel.

"It could take her over and we'll have no way of knowing."

She said before, if a Trilisk knows we're looking for it, it can avoid triggering our alarms.

"Then how do we know she's not already a Trilisk?" Magnus said.

Arakaki shook her head.

Two attendants awaited at the door for instructions. He told them to go in.

The door opened, and they flew inside. Magnus watched the feeds. One attendant hovered near the center of the bridge; the other flew for the vault room.

Magnus switched his attention to a feed from the second attendant. He saw the sapphire machine for one second; then the feed changed radically. The attendant had been transported into a nearby corridor. It reminded him of the attendants that had been ejected from the vine temple.

"That trick again," Arakaki said.

"I've tried envisioning that machine going back home," Telisa said. "It's not working."

"I was doing the same," Caden said.

"So much for praying to the AI, then," Siobhan said.

Magnus closed his eyes and imagined a rifle round sitting in one of his Veer pockets. After a few seconds, he reached in and pulled one out.

"The AI is working. It's still here," he said.

"I think it might be a robot that wants to go with the AI," Telisa said. "It's probably the same one we met in the complex."

"Great. It's immune to our weapons and it can teleport us away whenever it wants," Caden summarized.

"Then we're at an impasse," Marcant said.

"That's right. Consider, though, if it wanted us dead we'd be dead," Telisa said. "So there isn't much harm in me trying to approach it again."

And if it wants a host body, then it will grab you.

Magnus told himself it would have done that already, too. It wanted something else. He looked at Arakaki. She did not meet Magnus's gaze.

She sees this being fatal for all of us. A rerun of what happened to her before.

"Even with her at the aft of the ship, I think she's as close as we were when our host bodies were seized on the space habitat," Magnus said aloud to Arakaki.

"We're so helpless," she growled.

Magnus thought for another moment.

"Remember the grenade you used to wear around your neck?"

Arakaki looked back up and blinked.

"What?"

"Let me get a bigger grenade for you," he said.

"Telisa, stand by," he sent to Telisa as he asked for a channel to Sager and Arakaki.

"We have a situation here," Magnus said.

"What do you need, TM?" Sager asked.

"A Trilisk machine has appeared on our ship. We may become compromised. I want you to lock some capital ship firepower on us and stand by to fire at an instant's notice. Arakaki or I will be making the call," Magnus said.

To Sager's credit, there was only a moment of silence.

"You have it in fifteen seconds," Sager said.

"Thank you," Magnus said.

"Ready?" he asked Arakaki.

She nodded.

"Telisa. We've talked it over, and we're ready for you to go in and make contact with that thing."

"Good. I'm on my way."

A minute later Telisa walked back into the corridor. She stopped and dropped her weapons on the floor without saying anything, then walked past them and into the bridge.

Magnus watched her feed as she strode through the bridge over to the vault-arsenal corridor. She turned the corner and confronted the huge robot.

"Hello. Why are you here?" Telisa asked.

No answer came, at least none that Magnus could detect.

Telisa walked by the machine. It remained stationary.

"AI's still here. No sign of any other intruders," she said.

"There it is, then. It's guarding the AI, or at least following it for some reason," Magnus said.

"We'd better keep the battle spheres away from it," Telisa said. "We don't want a fight to break out between the pets."

"Can we really tolerate that thing in our ship? We're going to war," Magnus said.

"What choice do we have?" Telisa responded.

Magnus had no answer.

"It's coming with us whether we like it or not. At least Marcant can study it carefully."

"If it's like any other Trilisk technology, he won't get far," Magnus said.

"That's not a scientific attitude!" Marcant said. "But yes, you're right. We'll try anyway."

Michael McCloskey

Chapter 4

The combined Terran-Celaran fleet departed Celara Palnod on course for the enemy system the Cylerans had scouted. That system had been renamed Quarus Cora since no one knew for sure if it was their homeworld, but it had to pass for their equivalent of a Core World.

Telisa had been imagining ways to use the Trilisk AI for warfare. Since it was difficult to create complex structures via the AI, she had been keeping things simple. One of her schemes called for the creation of huge fields of ballistic material that could be accelerated toward Quarus targets.

A connection request dragged her from her work.

"Hello, Marcant."

"Hello. May I meet with you briefly? At your convenience."

Uh oh.

"Yes. Come on by in five."

"Thank you."

An old habit caused Telisa to glance about her quarters, looking for things to clean up before her guest arrived. She smiled. Her room was filled with weapons, artifacts, scanners and spare parts. There was no need to tidy anything. She wrapped up her virtual workspace and set it aside for further consideration later.

She half expected Marcant to bring in some device to test her humanity. After all, recent events had made everyone more paranoid about her host body problem.

Marcant signaled from the door.

"Come in," Telisa said.

Marcant walked in. He wore black. Telisa supposed he wanted to contrast his pale face. He carried a glucosoda as he often did. He looked at the can as if suddenly wondering if he should have brought it into the room.

It feels strange for anyone but Magnus to come into this room.

He looked her in the eye and spoke.

"I have to report that this project is a failure. Believe me, I'm taking it seriously, but we just don't have the traction to make progress."

"Are you talking about your study of the Trilisk robot, or screening the AI from arbitrary wishes?"

"Ah, sorry. I speak of the thought screening project."

"I appreciate your candor, Marcant. I'm disappointed, but not in you or your friends."

"I'm sorry to leave you in this position," Marcant said. "Without a thought screen, everyone will be able to draw upon the AI. What can we do?"

"We have to keep it a secret. That's the only solution I have right now. Some people in the fleet may notice, but I'm hoping if we keep our distance it won't be a major problem."

Marcant nodded.

"Adair will keep studying the Trilisk column in the Vovokan ship and the robot adjacent to the vault. Maybe there are clues there that could help with the AI. Achaius is learning about Vovokan software. What should I work on next?"

"Take your pick. We have a dozen mysteries lying around. Study Quarus technology, perhaps. I would stay away from Celaran study because Siobhan and Caden are on it. Plus, now that the Celarans are our friends, we can always cooperate with them to understand each other's systems with relatively little work."

"Okay. I'll learn something for sure. These other non-Trilisk technologies are within our grasp."

He turned and started to walk out.

"Marcant?"

Marcant turned back to face her. "Yes?"

"Can Adair and Achaius pray to the AI?"

"Yes," Marcant said. "Quite well, actually. They can produce more sophisticated things than I can."

Telisa nodded. "Good. Thank you."

Marcant nodded and left.

Do I trust them with the reins to the AI? If they can use it more effectively than I can, it could make the difference.

Telisa felt no surprise that his friends could use the artifact, even though the feat was amazing. If something could think, then the Trilisk AI could hear it and respond. The Trilisks were like gods to them. Had there been any wisdom behind that vast and staggering knowledge of theirs?

She hoped to find out before she died.

***

Sisela showed up early to warm up for her training session with the TM named Maxsym Kirilenko. She wore opaque undersheers and a light shirt since she did not know if Maxsym would work out in something thicker like a gi or not.

She did not know much about the man. He was a xenobiologist, a man who had heavily criticized the old Trilisk-dominated Core World government. Very little about his work with the PIT team was known. Some had attributed the anti-Trilisk toxin used in Space Force headquarters to him. Even though it made sense, Sisela did not know if it was true.

The *Sharplight*'s workout area was clean and spacious. It had areas with a softer floor for activities that involved throwing or falling and padded side rooms for pseudo-virtual training. Tucked away behind the mirrored walls sat heavy bag racks, training robots, and specialized exercise equipment.

Maxsym entered the large training area three minutes before their session was scheduled. The tall man wore durable hot-weather clothing. He carried a bag with him which had the looks of supplying other exercise accoutrements, even though there was a wall bin with almost anything he could need.

"TM Maxsym, right?"

"That's right," he said. "Nice to meet you. We're doing stand up today? I brought my Jiu Jitsu gi in case I misunderstood."

"Stand up is my thing, but I'm willing to trade with you straight across if you prefer to roll," she said. "Or throw."

"That won't be necessary," Maxsym said. "I need practice at everything. I have very little fast-twitch muscle, though. I'm going to assume that's not the case with you."

Sisela nodded. Somehow Maxsym had already made her feel like she was cheating just by having a superior fighting physique. She glanced at one of the spheres that orbited him.

"Those spheres are Vovokan?" Sisela asked. She knew the answer, but still felt curious about the alien machines.

"Yes. We call them attendants."

"So they do helpful little tasks for you?" Sisela guessed.

"Big tasks, too," Maxsym said. "They could even defend me against you. Which is why I have to shoo them away so we can spar."

"Amazing. Super useful."

Maxsym dismissed his attendants. They floated away off the soft area of the floor.

They squared off. Sisela probed his defenses with light strikes. He hard-blocked one roundhouse and deflected another to pass by. She launched a slow side kick at his midriff and he dropped his arm to hook it away.

Sisela mixed in punches with her kicks. Maxsym continued to deflect her attacks without counter. He concentrated only on defense. At least he seemed to know multiple techniques to defend himself: hard blocks, soft deflections and timed retreats.

Sisela started to put some pop into her attacks. The top of her foot smacked his short ribs and when he dropped his arm, she landed another across his temple. Maxsym did not lose his focus or his cool. He covered and retreated.

Maxsym weathered the first ten-minute round about as well as she did, but he had gone without the extra exertion of constantly attacking. They took a break by the side of the combat area.

It was clear to Sisela that Maxsym was of intermediate skill in hand-to-hand.

This wasn't a trap. Telisa just had me start at the bottom.

"You can attack, right?" she asked politely.

"I can attack a heavybag," Maxsym said. He smiled.

"Do the other team members encourage you to try out a more aggressive style?"

Maxsym smiled. "They know I'm a xenobiologist who prefers to stay out of the combat zone, so most of them cut me some slack. But Arakaki and Telisa both have me under pressure to start attacking."

"Then this is the perfect time to get your feet wet. I attacked you for an entire round and you took it. Let's switch. I'll hold my counters and you can come after me this next round."

Maxsym nodded.

"Thank you," he said.

"Pace yourself," she warned as they walked back out into the middle.

Maxsym nodded. He moved forward, launching some jabs. Sisela circled away, first to the left and then suddenly switching to the right. Maxsym came after her. To his credit, he started to string his attacks into combinations of three or four techniques.

Soon he was breathing heavily and slowing down. After seven minutes, he was no longer able to launch a respectable attack, so Sisela dropped her defense.

"Let's take a break," she said. "You're not used to that."

Maxsym nodded, trying to catch his breath. A bench folded out of the wall for them to sit down on.

"So how is the ship working? Everything in order?" Maxsym asked between puffs. Sisela wondered if he was simply being polite, or asking to give himself more time to recover.

Or maybe he's genuinely curious about it, she decided.

"Actually, the ship is working better than should be possible," she said. "I reported everything to Telisa, since I have orders to report anomalies. She didn't seem surprised."

"That may be due to some special technology the team uses," Maxsym said between gulps of air.

"Oh? I wondered. Whatever it is, it's amazing. I swear some of the laws of physics are being broken."

"It might be the side effects of alien technology," suggested Maxsym again. "As long as you keep Telisa informed, it should be fine."

"I will. By the way, I don't know if I'm supposed to ask this, but why the lockdown the other day? I was confined to quarters and the entire ship was on a security alert."

"A drill?" Maxsym said. "I don't know. I was on the Vovokan *Iridar*. I have important work there."

"Ah, right."

Maxsym stripped down to his undersheers and stepped into a recessed shower that opened in the mirrored wall. Sisela glanced at him and saw he was fit, though covered in bruises which stood out on his pale skin. He washed the sweat off in about twenty seconds and let the shower dry him. Sisela did not follow suit even though there were other shower niches nearby.

"How're your other combat skills?" Sisela asked him when he emerged.

"Very good," he said. "I've killed several Trilisks."

"Really? Projectile or energy weapons?"

"Neither. I made the poison gas that killed them."

Sisela laughed.

"Okay, okay, you get credit for that!" she said. "Whatever gets the job done, man."

"Thank you for the workout. I'll see you next time."

"See you."

Sisela told a heavybag to drop from the ceiling. A large red body-weight bag descended and began circling her. Sisela launched well-timed attacks on the moving target, putting her full power into them. Fifteen minutes passed as she danced with the training device until she received a notification that Marcant had arrived.

She turned to see him walking in. He was shorter than Maxsym and even paler. He wore a thin gi which, despite its light construction, was probably extremely durable. He had brought a small drink container, which was odd, since the gym had water sources behind the mirrors of the wall.

She mentally shrugged. *To each his own.*

"TM Marcant," Sisela greeted him. It felt like a rerun of an hour ago.

"Marcant is fine," he said quickly.

"You can call me Barrai if you like," she said. "You know, in the Force most of us go by our last names."

"Got it. Actually, Marcant is my last name, too. I was never in the Space Force, though... I just go by my last name as well."

She nodded.

"Looks like you've been working out already. That's good for me," Marcant said.

Sisela smiled.

"I saw that my access had been cut back."

"Yes. We have to maintain a high level of security," Marcant said. "Tell you what. I won't take this beating personally if you don't take your access restrictions personally."

Sisela smiled. "Deal. Hey, why the lockdown the other day?"

"Telisa is always doing drills and training exercises, both virtual and real," Marcant said. "I'm sure you know all about it, given the Space Force training you likely still undergo every day."

Marcant walked out onto the floor and began his warmup. He hopped around and did some rolls while Sisela ran a circuit of the gym, then they started to spar.

Marcant immediately stood out as having a radically different style than Maxsym. When Sisela attacked with light jabs or kicks to his front leg, he countered aggressively though without proper timing.

At least he's trying to counter, but he's just not very good at it.

Sisela attacked rapidly. Marcant tried to absorb the punishment and counter, so Sisela put more power into her strikes. She felt that taking a hit to dish one out was sometimes a valid strategy, but she wanted to remind Marcant that it came with painful drawbacks. Marcant made it through the first ten minutes, steadily declining in performance.

They took a break. A fan vent opened in the floor and created an airflow off to one side. Marcant walked into the column of fast-moving air to cool off.

"How do you like the *Sharplight*?" Sisela asked as he recovered.

"I like it. But I like the other two *Iridars* as well."

"Our ships are removed from the rest of the fleet," Sisela said. "Shouldn't we be closer for our own safety?"

"Oh. I think it's because we dabble in dangerous alien technologies," Marcant said. "Telisa is quite altruistic. I think she's protecting the fleet, not the other way around."

I wonder if that's true. Maybe what I've been seeing really is alien tech at work!

They fought for two more long rounds. Marcant did not give up his assaults. She wondered if Maxsym was his usual sparring partner and this is how they fit together: Marcant always attacking and Maxsym always defending. That would leave them both in a rut. She decided they must be doing all manner of training with the rest of the team as well. Her imagined scenario probably occurred, but it could not be totally accurate.

At the end of their third round, Marcant struggled to hold up his hands in surrender.

"I'm sorry, Barrai. I've had enough for today," he gasped, staggering away.

"Take deep, controlled breaths," she said. "Fill the bottom of your lungs first, from your belly."

Marcant flopped down onto a wall bench. He reached for his drink container.

"Why?" he asked.

"To get the oxygen into your system. Use all of your lungs to maximize oxygen uptake."

"Why would breathing from the diaphragm do that? My normal fight-or-flight response breathing should maximize oxygen uptake. Why would we have evolved to breathe inefficiently under physical stress?"

Barrai did a double-take. She grasped for an answer.

"Most Core Worlders don't exercise, so they don't breathe correctly."

"That's my point... we breathe instinctively. Why would that be the inefficient way?"

"Maybe while you're running or fighting, you can't take time to breathe in deeply, but now the workout is over, so you have to force yourself to change your breathing."

"I don't buy it. Who told you to do that?"

"Martial arts instructors—"

"Exactly. And what do they like? Discipline. They tell you what to do and you do it, you don't question it. The result, we have people breathing deeply from the bottom of their lungs up for thousands of years because some teacher way back at the beginning wanted his students to hide how far into oxygen debt they were in a fight. To breathe hard was a sign of weakness, told the enemy they were tiring out. But he never told them *why* to do that. He just said *do* it."

Barrai felt herself bristle a bit at his tone, but she remained calm.

"Martial things are for fighting. So discipline is required because there is a chain of command. If students or soldiers are always bickering with their commanders, that's dangerous for everyone."

"Fair enough. I agree about the discipline. But right now, I want to know *why* it would be better to fill the bottom of my lungs first rather than breathing as I naturally do."

"Well... there are a lot of natural things that are not optimal, right?" she asked.

"Not optimal along our desired artificial axes, perhaps. But optimal for survival and reproduction, likely."

"I'll try to find out the answer for you."

"Maxsym is our man. He'll tell us."

Barrai nodded. She made a note to herself to look into the matter, though she was interested to hear what Maxsym might have to say. Marcant was simply abrasive. She tried to tell herself she did not feel annoyed because he questioned her advice; it was because of *how* he had done it. Or was it?

"Thank you for the workout," Sisela told him coldly.

"No need to thank me, it wasn't my idea," Marcant said.

"Oh? You were *ordered* to train with me?"

Marcant stood awkwardly still for a moment, then said, "Normally that doesn't happen. It might be that it was punishment for failing a recent project."

First Marcant smiled as if the explanation somehow made it sound better. Then he seemed to sense that he had misspoken to her.

"It's good for me to endure physical hardship," he said. "I'm supposed to become... more durable..." his voice trailed off.

"Well, thank you anyway," Sisela said.

Marcant looked relieved that she had accepted his answers.

"I'll see you later," he said and hurried off.

"Okay."

She headed for one of the showers as he left the gym.

"The PIT team: mysterious, as expected. And *eccentric*," she told her log.

***

Maxsym hurried back to the lab on the *Iridar* to resume his work with Ms. Stalos.

"You're back!" Stracey said enthusiastically. "I have one thousand host neural samples ready to bombard. If they react as they've done in the simulations, we'll know the Stenning Supposition is worth following up on."

"Wonderful. I wish I could have been here."

Maxsym tried to refocus on the task at hand. The short exercise session had made him feel refreshed mentally, though his body ached.

"How did your fighting go?"

Maxsym shrugged. "Well enough. I fought a Space Force officer."

"Really? Not a TM?"

She seems very interested. Why?

"Not this time. It was a new person. She's very skilled. Much better than me."

"Oh, I'm sure you're being modest," Stracey said. She looked directly at him with her beautiful liquid eyes.

Maxsym suddenly felt a bit giddy under her intense gaze. Stracey's physical presence was powerful; she was also incredibly intelligent. Finally, she looked like Telisa, which was having an additional effect on him.

He could not find words, so he pulled up the sleeve of his disposable lab garment and showed her a bruise on his forearm by way of proof.

"Oh!" she said, stepping close. She reached out and touched his arm near the bruise. Then her hand slid smoothly up and felt his triceps brachii.

"There are a lot of strong, intelligent men in GNI. I see them every day. But they're all toning pills and cardio machine training. Not like you. You're so... real, Maxsym. You're a pioneer in your field, and, literally, in the field... beyond the frontier!"

She pressed against him. He felt his heart leap in his chest. Maxsym was mesmerized.

"It would be irresponsible to..." he mumbled.

"To have sex on the job? Or have sex *in the lab?*" she asked quickly.

Maxsym's resistance gave way. He tore open the green lab smock covering her torso and gloried at what was revealed.

Chapter 5

Arakaki swam submerged through warm water. Her Veer suit provided oxygen and protection. There was no surface above her, only the smooth blue ceiling of a Quarus spacecraft. She kept her streamlined weapon ready before her. If any enemy appeared within a 20-degree firing cone, the weapon could lock on and hit in less than a second without any need for her to further align it on target.

The team approached a tricky choke point in the simulation. All the scouting devices they had sent ahead had died past the narrowing of the ship between a power generation station and its crew section. Arakaki, leading the exercise in lieu of Telisa, sent Caden and Siobhan to the left and motioned for Magnus and Marcant to take the right.

Arakaki noted the ceiling rose half again higher than usual at the juncture. A corridor perhaps 4 meters wide extended upward about 8 meters. The sides were smooth ceramic.

"Each side, split your coverage vertically."

Within a couple of seconds, Caden and Marcant had shifted their weapons accordingly.

"I'm going forward to check it out," Arakaki said.

"They'll be waiting for you," Magnus warned.

"We need something out of the box," Caden added.

"I'm all ears."

No one replied. Arakaki adjusted her ballast causing herself to rise to the ceiling. She inched forward. The psychological change of looking at the intersection from above instead of the floor was considerable. Now Arakaki felt like a sniper ready to pick off something unawares.

Water dwellers probably experience this very differently. A height advantage is not worth as much in water as it is in air, so Quarus instincts would not produce this feeling of power from an elevation.

Arakaki forced herself to evaluate the situation objectively as she drifted past the narrowest point in the choke. The area beyond had no cover. Even worse, three long corridors emptied into the atrium, so they could be taking fire from different directions at once. Arakaki looked for sensors but she could not see anything obvious. She knew that did not mean much; even at a Terran level of technology, interior sensors could be visible or invisible depending on what the builders intended.

"I don't see them but I suspect they want to lead us all into this kill zone. I'm sending an attendant ahead."

"They'll just kill it," Caden said.

Arakaki knew he was right, but what could they do?

A vent on her left caught her attention. She would never have looked at it closely from below, but from the ceiling, she could see deeply into it. There was no room for a Terran or Celaran, but an attendant could negotiate the narrow waterway if she pulled out one of the vent flaps.

"Hang on. These vents are large enough for an attendant!"

"Ah, nice. We could get behind them and spy from there," Siobhan said.

Arakaki swam over to the vent. She reached into her pack for a mechanical fastener.

Ha. A smart rope would do nicely, but we have none for underwater missions.

Arakaki had found a waterproof tools case when her attendant alerted her to a glimpse of motion from the far right. Arakaki played it back: a half-centimeter of chitinous leg had briefly been exposed. Her underwater listening device reported motion waves coming from first one, then all the corridors.

"They're coming! A lot of them!" Caden said from beyond the choke.

"I'm falling back," Arakaki said. She pushed hard off the ceiling and pointed her weapon back the way she had come. A quick link command activated its water jet, causing the torpedo-shaped weapon to pull her through the water back toward safety. She felt exposed.

These things are fast, but not faster than a Quarus laser!

Arakaki dropped a bubbler as she passed back through the narrowest point. It uncoiled below her and emitted swarms of CO_2 bubbles which rose to form a "wall" across the corridor to cover her escape and her team's positions. Arakaki glanced back as she headed for the nearest corner. The bubbles scintillated as beam weapons split up in the visible spectrum as it they passed through. Popping sounds accentuated the white noise of her bubbler as the lasers caused small sonic emanations where the energy vaporized water.

"Stay set up here," Arakaki said, stating the obvious. The choke point would work both ways. "Is everyone all right?"

"My membrane is broken," Siobhan reported. "It must have happened when we took out that guard machine at the waterlock."

"Got you covered," Arakaki said.

Arakaki triggered a timer in her PV to track Siobhan's estimated oxygen levels. Even though they each carried oxygen separator membrane on their backs, the team had become proficient at sharing oxygen on timed intervals for situations like this.

Arakaki's link received a fatigue warning from the bubbler she had dropped. Three seconds later, the bubbler ran out of CO_2 to emit. The stream abruptly ended and the last of the bubbles rose.

"Targets!" Caden transmitted.

Arakaki aligned her weapon to cover the way through the choke. The combo weapon had two very different modes of attack. The first was a water frequency laser, which Arakaki thought of as a "laser shotgun" because it could not hurt a minnow at a range of 30 meters. The other part of the weapon fired low-caliber flechette rounds which delivered a toxin developed by Maxsym for Quarus targets. The long, thin flechettes carried well through the water compared to normal rounds, but the water was too dense; they offered barely any more range than the laser. The Quarus, being native water dwellers and possessing more advanced technology, had better lasers with limited effects out to 50 meters.

Sadly, one of the PIT team's shortest-range air weapons, the breaker claws, were their longest range underwater weapon, roughly matching the range of the Quarus lasers. For better or for worse, having a wall of water between oneself and the enemy only made it harder to harm each other.

Arakaki had an open connection to her weapon and was ready to use it.

Four massive shapes cut through the water toward the team's position. Arakaki used her breaker claw.

Krumpf. Krumpf.

Two of the objects burst at the same time. Bubbles erupted from the heat of shorted systems.

A dozen lasers drove her team back under cover. The remaining two machines crossed the choke and fired. The team shot back.

Tink tink tink tink tink.

Scratches appeared on one machine's casing, but the tiny flechettes were not enough to harm it.

Caden grunted in surprise and pain on the channel. Arakaki's link made her aware he had been hit, but she did not have the time to follow up.

Marcant lit up the nearest machine by dumping his laser's full charge into it. The last machine broke apart in a burst of bubbles as someone else got it with a breaker claw.

Sizzle. Brumf.

"There's more coming!" Marcant warned.

Arakaki reached into her pack, but Magnus was ahead of her. He had already taken out a grenade. The seeking weapon looked like a mini-torpedo. He launched it a second later.

Foooooosh.

The torpedo accelerated toward the Quarus as they moved across the atrium. A couple of Quarus were injured as the team used breaker claws on their weapons, causing the power rings to explode. Then the powered grenade arrived and detonated.

Crack. Crack. Kwump!

Each soft target took a spike of poisoned metal as well as the shock wave in the first second. Arakaki felt the compression wave hit her the next, but the torpedo did not send as much energy back the way it had come, so she easily absorbed it. Their attackers broke into soft masses of red goop. Their armored legs broke off and slowly settled downward.

So much bright red blood filled the water that Arakaki could not see the atrium beyond the choke point.

"I'm sending another grenade in blind," Arakaki announced, launching her own mini-torpedo into the bloody mess before them.

Kwump!

It exploded amid the cloud and reported four more probable kills.

Arakaki received an end-of-scenario pointer.

"End simulation," she said and pulled out of the virtual world.

Michael McCloskey

Everyone opened their eyes in the big meeting room. The curved walls showed random scenes piped in from Celara Palnod. Some centered on Space Force relief teams, others displayed Celaran scouts flying through the forest.

"They're getting harder," Caden noted out loud.

"That blood really shuts our detection down," Arakaki said. "I bet the Quarus have submarine equivalents of smoke grenades that will limit our vision. They probably also have sonar equipment that can see through it."

"I'm still working on the sonar modules for the attendants," Magnus said. "It will give them away, but they're expendable."

Arakaki nodded.

"The Quarus must be able to scatter sonar signals," Caden said. "They've doubtless fought wars against each other in their distant past. By now, they must have developed something to render sonar signals useless."

"Well I hope we don't have to do anything as crazy as going up against their soldiers underwater," Siobhan said.

Arakaki agreed with the sentiment. The current simulations were dialed back from the expected effectiveness of real Quarus soldiers to match the PIT team's current abilities. They were now certain that the Quarus they had faced on the space station had been scientists and their robots, not a military unit.

"We won't have to. We have the AI," Marcant said.

"How are we going to use it though? Just wish the Quarus to lose?" Siobhan.

"Maybe we could pray up a peace treaty they would agree to," Caden said.

"That would be harder than you think," Siobhan said. "Remember how detailed we have to be? Even for small things."

"Yes it might be very difficult," Arakaki agreed. "Even when I prayed together a combat machine that I knew every piece of, it took hours; and it still wasn't quite right."

"We don't know its real limitations," Magnus said. "But I think we're going to find out. It has to be powerful if one can make everyone on Earth happy."

"Sisela is coming," Siobhan hissed.

Arakaki looked over to see that Sisela was indeed approaching. She was not too surprised, since the team had decided to leave their restricted decks for this session. Sisela would naturally be curious.

"TMs," Sisela said carefully.

"Lieutenant," Arakaki answered.

"I'm guessing you're doing some VR training," Sisela said. "Got space for another? I can play any role you need, good guy or bad."

"Sorry, but our training is closed to outsiders, even Space Force personnel," Arakaki said firmly.

"You guys don't usually do this off the restricted decks, do you? I haven't seen you around."

Meaning, she hasn't gotten an alert that we left the restricted area before.

"Change of scenery," Siobhan said.

Sisela nodded.

"Then I'll take off," Sisela said. She spoke politely but in that manner that said between the lines, '*I don't really want to*'.

"You don't have to. We're done for this shift," Siobhan said.

Caden hopped up with Siobhan and they stretched. Siobhan laid a leg onto the meeting table and grabbed her foot.

Arakaki noted that Siobhan avoided her gaze. Siobhan had not said anything to her today. Even Caden only threw nervous glances her way.

I guess it's that she's sensitive about me being around Caden.

Arakaki tried to remember the last time she had been territorial about a guy or a girl. She immediately regretted it. She would never feel that way again. She bit down hard on the sliver in her mouth.

Get over it already. You've trained yourself to be overly dramatic when it comes to some things.

Arakaki wanted to shed it all like old skin. But something inside her was still knotted up. She decided to go for a run around the ship to distract herself.

"We could run," Arakaki blurted, looking toward Sisela.

Sisela looked surprised.

"Hell yeah. Let's do it."

Arakaki pulled the sliver out of her mouth and slipped it into a knot in the smart string around her neck. Sisela took note but said nothing.

The two of them ran toward the longest perimeter corridor, a special walkway designed for exercise as well as normal movement through the ship. Once on the soft track, they picked up the pace to a fast but sustainable run.

"So who's hooked up with who around here?" Sisela asked.

So much for getting away from that.

"You ask as many questions as a spy," Arakaki said mildly.

Sisela did not answer right away.

"Nope, there's nothing you can say to prove you're not one if you're not, or to deflect my suspicions if you are," Arakaki said.

"True," Sisela said. "I admire the PIT team like everyone else. I really felt honored when all my hard work paid off with this assignment. So I ask questions. I'd be stupid if I let the opportunity to learn pass by."

Arakaki nodded. They turned a sharp corner. The pressure on her feet to accelerate sharply left felt good.

"Telisa has a thing with Magnus," Arakaki said. "Doesn't everyone on Sol know that?"

"Yes and no. I mean, there are countless rumors and that's a popular one, but when it comes to the PIT team, you just don't know what's true and what isn't."

"Everything's that way. No one can really tell what's true unless they check it themselves. If you take someone's word for it on the net, you fall for their agenda."

"Well now I have it on good authority," Sisela said.

"Then there's Siobhan and Caden."

"Oh! Really? That would break a lot of hearts," Sisela laughed.

"Siobhan is popular?"

"No! Caden! He's a superstar. His Blood Glades footage has been watched almost as much as all those big parties at Stark's."

It felt strange to gossip with the Space Force officer. Not only because she was ex-UED, but also because Arakaki was usually always on-mission.

"And me?"

"Everyone thinks you're dead! I was so surprised to see you."

"Reports of my death are highly exaggerated."

"What? Oh, right!"

"It's something Maxsym said," Arakaki told her. "I figured it came from some historical reference, but I guess you aren't familiar with it either."

Sisela shook her head.

They ran for a long time, and Arakaki did manage to forget about her pain.

Michael McCloskey

Chapter 6

The fleet came to station well outside the most distant of six planets in the target system which had been called Quarus Cora in the strategy documents, even though it was not clear if that was in fact the Quarus home system. Celaran and Terran experts had come up with the distance they felt confident would avoid early detection.

It now fell upon them to make the last preparations for the assault from beyond the outer system.

Telisa watched from the bridge lounge as a shared system map filled with refreshed information from their sensors and a network of cloaked probes.

"Marcant? Can we see anything from out this far?"

"Yes. The defenses are even denser than we thought. I can see significant numbers of satellites, presumably defense hardware, even beyond that asteroid belt."

"Anything else?"

"There are active signals being sent from several locations to observe the outer system."

"My officers assure me that we've been able to absorb and scatter enough of the energy that they won't be getting any echoes off us," Sager chimed in.

"Keep looking and planning. Is there a corridor into there that would let us avoid a good part of the defenses?"

"We could approach outside the plane of the planets and the belt, but that has its own disadvantages. First, they've planned for that by placing these groups of stations here and here. Also, we would be the target of a simultaneous retaliation wave from many bases in the planetary plane. Either way, this is grim."

Telisa had heard similar analyses from the Space Force admirals. Clearing the belt or a part of it would deny resources to the inner planets and deprive the Quarus of many of their bases from which they might launch attacks on the invading fleet.

"Then I'd better get started," Telisa said.

***

Telisa regarded the massive Trilisk machine before her. Its three legs folded up close to its body in the relatively narrow corridor. It had three arms, offset evenly between the three legs, also folded in the confining space. The body was a smooth, elegant tetrahedron.

Basically an artificial Trilisk body. Presumably with an artificial mind, not a real Trilisk brain?

Maxsym and Marcant had spent time during the voyage trying to scan the machine and discover if it held a biological brain inside, but their results were inconclusive. Telisa supposed that even if a Trilisk did live inside that body, it would not need its consciousness to sit inside of a biological mind anyway.

Telisa wondered how old it was. Had this device been constructed when the Trilisks ruled the Orion Arm of the galaxy? That led her to a wild theory: what if there had been a Trilisk brain in there and it had died of old age? The machine could be walking around on autopilot.

The Trilisks must have achieved immortality at their peak. They can transfer snapshots of a consciousness into alien minds.

"I'm going to communicate with the AI up close," she told it. Even though the machine had never responded to anything she said, she wanted to let it know what was going on in case it understood and cared.

Marcant had expressed a concern that being anywhere near the machine was dangerous because it might 'figure out' that Telisa was not a Trilisk in a host body. She found that worry valid, but she had put it aside because she refused to allow fear to paralyze the team.

At least that was what she told Marcant. Maybe the real reason she kept interacting with the robot was that she could not turn off her intense curiosity about the Trilisks, their robot, or the reason for its presence. The ideas churned through her head: It could be a beacon, calling Trilisks to the AI, in which case the team was probably doomed. Or it could be a guardian of the device, or even a mentor for those who would use it.

She walked beyond the machine and approached the AI. She knew she did not have to be close in order to use it, at least not if it was like the others, but she felt being closer might help somehow. She thought that close-proximity prayers might overpower distant ones. Would being closer give a stronger signal and get her requests the priority they needed to succeed?

Magnus linked in from his quarters to control a small group of attendants outside the ship. The attendants pulled a Space Force missile out a half kilometer from the ship and then returned.

"There's your first one," Magnus said. "I've turned off all sensors in bay three. Hopefully that's where we can get our new ones."

Telisa focused a bank of ship's sensors onto the missile and brought it into clear focus in her personal view. The dart-shaped object was the size of a person. Such weapons were designed so that their launch could be boosted by an asymmetric pattern in a ship's gravity spinner. Even so, the weapons were limited to sublight velocities since they carried no spinner of their own. If one were launched by a ship moving too fast, the missile would drop back into normal space and likely explode in the transition.

I want another one in bay three. An exact copy of that one. It has to be exactly the same, though. So important. This is really needed badly and it has to be the same in every way.

"Okay, take a peek."

Magnus reactivated the sensors in bay three. At the center lay a new Space Force missile.

"Check that one please," Telisa transmitted. Attendants flitted over and scanned the weapon. There was a delay of a second or two as Magnus looked over the results.

"It's good," he reported.

"Great. Now a bigger batch," she said.

They shut down the sensors and repeated the procedure.

I need more. All the same. They have to all work exactly the same way.

The sensors snapped back on. This time the bay had ten missiles in it.

Hrm. Why ten? I guess that's a lot more than before. Did the AI intuit my notion of an order of magnitude? Would a Trilisk have gotten three, nine, or twenty seven of them?

"An improvement," Magnus said, though he sounded as puzzled as her.

"Again," Telisa said. She waited until the feed of the bay went dead, then started to concentrate.

I need that bay full of these. Exactly like the ones I have. We need perfect duplicates and a lot of them. It's very important.

"Okay, check it," Telisa told Magnus.

In the bay, they saw three new missiles.

"What's up?" Magnus asked.

"Something's wrong," Telisa said.

"Surely it has no limitation on... repetition?" Magnus sent her, thinking out loud.

"Well it is an alien device. Have we ever prayed up lots of something before?"

"I made a lot of robot parts once," Magnus said. "I'm pretty sure I made more than this. But those parts were smaller."

"It worked as expected at first. It seems fatigued," Telisa said.

"How can it already be fatigued? Is this one broken?" he asked.

"Bored?"

"Bored! I would laugh, but..."

"Maybe it's too old. I don't know," Telisa said. "If we can't scale up the duplication, I can't even make a field of ball bearings to accelerate at the Quarus satellites."

This is a major setback. We may have to call this entire attack off.

"Let's try some more," Telisa said.

Magnus pulled the hardware from the bay and shut down the sensors again.

I need a vast quantity of those missiles. Just like the last ones, exactly like them. We need them badly.

Once again, they found three new missiles.

"They check out," Magnus reported. "As far as I can tell, all these missiles will be effective."

Telisa pulled a small, dense sphere from a pocket and felt its weight in her hands. She lapsed into thought.

Ball bearings. Surround that missile outside with tiny tungsten balls.

Telisa imagined Magnus's sample missile surrounded by hundreds of tiny spheres. The spheres did not need to be ferrous to be used for an attack since they could use the gravity spinner to launch them instead of a magnetic field.

"Check the first missile," Telisa asked. "What do we have out there?"

"I see some tungsten objects. Ten of them. Very small," he noted.

"What's wrong?" Telisa asked. "We made so many things before..."

"I'm still guessing it's broken. Or a lesser model," Magnus said.

"Emergency FTF meeting. 10 minutes," she announced on the team channel. She connected to Maxsym on the Vovokan *Iridar*. "Maxsym, you don't have to show up incarnate for this, just be on the channel, okay?"

"Absolutely."

Telisa walked to a secure meeting room on deck 11, one of the PIT-restricted decks. She met Lee and Magnus there. The meeting room's walls changed to a projection of a Celaran vine jungle. The room now resembled one of the balconies on the Celaran house they had lived in briefly.

Caden, Siobhan, and Marcant joined them. Arakaki hurried in last, wearing only undersheers and a light shirt. Her skin glistened and her hair was wet. She must have walked right out of the shower tube and into the meeting room. A dark look crossed Siobhan's face when she saw Arakaki.

Don't have time for that issue.

"Since we arrived, Magnus and I began production of weapons using the AI. We quickly discovered that the AI isn't operating at full capacity," Telisa said aloud, though her speech also went out on the team channel for Maxsym. "We didn't even get twenty of them."

"You tried several times?" Siobhan asked.

"Yes. It will only make them three at a time now," Telisa told them. "The biggest batch I got was ten. I also tried to create a huge field of tungsten pellets, but we only got a few. What could be wrong?"

"First let's compile a list of things that have changed," Marcant suggested. "We're using a different AI than before. We're on a different ship. We're in a different system."

"We don't have the harness," Siobhan said. "Maybe other people are stealing all your juice."

"That one sounds likely. Other possibilities?" Telisa asked.

"The robot. Could it be interfering, or could it be using power?" Caden asked.

"Good point. Okay, anything else change?"

"You're a host body, but that should help, not hinder," Magnus said.

Telisa nodded.

"Shiny was with us before," Arakaki said. "Maybe the bastard knows lots of secrets to making the AI work well and he never shared them with us."

That hypothesis gave Telisa pause because it seemed plausible and sounded like something Shiny would do.

The comments stopped.

"Keep thinking. More possibilities, please," Telisa said.

"We're way outside the system," Maxsym said. "Maybe the AI needs starlight. Or maybe it steals power from the star some other way and it needs to be closer."

Marcant looked intrigued by the idea. Telisa nodded. It was worth considering.

"Maybe it doesn't like us or our vine," Lee suggested. "It has to be smart to do what it does? Do you think it has a personality?"

"We don't know," Telisa said.

"I don't think it's like Achaius and Adair," Marcant said. Everyone paid close attention at the rare mention of his companions. "I suspect that the Trilisks made a utility that fulfilled a wide variety of needs quickly and easily. I don't think it has wants or needs of its own."

"We have a long list of possibilities," Telisa said. "I'm troubled by how few we can change, though. This is the only AI we have, and I don't know if we can get rid of the robot. That could be its purpose, though. It might be here to police usage of the AI."

"Maybe Shiny's AI had one too, and he figured out a way to 'dispose' of it," Magnus said.

"I can check with Sager and make sure there aren't any Space Force personnel praying things up, whether or not they know what they're doing," Magnus said.

"Yes. Has anyone here been making a lot of stuff with the AI?" Telisa asked. "We should put an eye on Barrai, too, and make sure she's not doing something crazy, even though she doesn't know about it. Or at least, I hope she hasn't learned about it."

"I've only made small things. A new sleep web, some small amenities," Siobhan said.

"Same here," Caden said.

Arakaki shrugged. Magnus shook his head.

"Have Adair or Achaius been using the Trilisk AI much?" Telisa asked.

Marcant shook his head. "A few experiments to see what they could accomplish. Nothing at scale like you're attempting."

"Maxsym. Does Stracey know about the AI?"

"Not that I know of," he said. "I've used the AI to help with some samples. Microscopic things. I can't imagine it draining much, but I'll stop anyway."

"Lee? Been praying much?"

"Since we put all the vines in my room, I've created only four ring batteries for my tool rods," Lee said.

"Well we're not getting much closer to the star, not with all that Quarus hardware in-system," Caden pointed out. "So the idea about our position so far out of the system is hard to test."

"Yes, but I think that's the right idea," Arakaki said. "I don't mean starlight, exactly, because that's not much energy compared to what it must need. But the power to run that thing comes from somewhere, and if it's not getting enough, that would explain it."

"Well if it did use starlight, something as advanced as that would not rely just upon the starlight that falls on its surface," Marcant offered. "It would probably harvest a much larger area of incidence. We could put out a net of attendants and have them measure the star's light at various positions beyond the AI. They might be able to detect if it's harvesting that energy."

"We'll follow up on the rogue usage angle," Telisa said. "Otherwise, we're in trouble. We have to get to the bottom of this or this fight is going to be devastating for this fleet."

She did not say the rest: If the Trilisk AI could not be leveraged well, it might be best to call off the assault altogether.

Michael McCloskey

Chapter 7

Magnus attended a fleet meeting with Telisa. They sat in a meeting room, this time just the two of them, while the other participants linked in from other ships. Magnus set them to overlay his real vision so he saw them seated around the table as if they were present incarnate. The virtual forms of Admiral Sager, Cynan, and two Celaran leaders appeared before him.

The two Celaran leaders immediately destroyed the illusion. Wherever they were, they were flying, so their virtual forms wriggled almost comically. Magnus shrugged.

I guess Celarans don't sit still for meetings.

Admiral Sager looked like he wanted to start. Telisa delayed for a few long moments, then spoke first.

"The fleet is in position. However, I would like to delay the first stage of our campaign here. Unless we see evidence that we've been discovered, of course."

Magnus watched Sager's lips compress. Something was wrong.

"Our fleet looks insufficient to challenge the Quarus in this system," one of the Celaran leaders said. "Many flew here with us, but our enemies have not stopped building defenses on their vines."

"I concur," Cynan said. "We should consider a reduced response from our previous plan. We could destroy their presence in the asteroid belt and declare it to be our retribution for the attack on Celara Palnod. That would serve to show them our alliance in action, which was one of the goals."

Something changed. Did her influence wear off? Or is the AI sick?

Magnus looked to Sager. The Terran Admiral felt the same way, he decided, but would not speak before Telisa asked for his opinion.

59

Michael McCloskey

"I'm working on something that will give us the edge back," Telisa said. "Please give me a few more days. We've come this far; I can show you a method to bring us victory with significantly fewer losses."

"If you have such capability, why have you not unveiled it to all who hang here?" asked a Celaran commander. "Why is it not part of the plan for our bright day?"

"I wasn't able to deploy some of the technology at my disposal until we arrived. It takes time to prepare. Please be patient. If this does not work out, then I'll agree to your suggested reduction in the scope of our operation here."

She'll never let that happen, Magnus thought. *We didn't come this far to bow out early.*

"Tell us what this tool or tools are, if we must share a dangerous vine, then we deserve to know," said the Celaran leader who had been silent until now.

Damn. It's a fair request!

Telisa managed to keep her face calm, though Magnus knew she must be struggling.

"It's a secret, so please don't let this information go beyond the six of us," Telisa said. "We have a Trilisk tool. Powerful beyond anything our civilizations yet have."

The Celarans responded with a play of lights across their backs. Magnus hoped that no other Celarans would observe whatever they might be saying, if it was about the Trilisk weapon.

"I suggest a compromise, then," Cynan said. "We will plan for a campaign against this belt only. If you show us that the tool is as powerful as you claim, then we may decide to continue the campaign from there."

"That sounds reasonable," a Celaran commander chimed in. "Stay on a juicy vine for half a day and see if the weather turns."

"Thank you," Telisa said. "That does sound reasonable. We can strike in a few days."

"We will wait for a bright day, then," a Celaran said.

The Celarans signed off the channel. Cynan and Sager remained.

"The Terrans are assigned 70% of the belt targets," Cynan said. "If you manage to use your alien tool successfully, you should complete the objectives ahead of schedule. You can save us losses by then sending along elements of your fleet to help us with ours. That will increase the chances of continuing the campaign."

"We will," Telisa assured him. Cynan dropped the channel.

"Is there anything I can do to help, TM?" Sager said.

"Yes. Don't tell Shiny that we have this Trilisk tool," Telisa said. "And if he finds out, lead him to believe it's not Trilisk in nature."

Hrm. Telisa is going to press his loyalties here. But I think he knows her better than he knows Shiny, and besides, she's Terran.

Admiral Sager looked unhappy indeed. Telisa continued.

"We have work to do on this end to make this succeed. We'll keep you updated."

Telisa cut the connection and Admiral Sager's avatar disappeared.

"No pressure," Magnus said.

Telisa sighed. Magnus let her keep thinking. He opened a channel with Marcant.

"We just met with our allies. They're skittish," Magnus said.

"The alliance is new and fragile, eh?"

"How does the situation look to you, Marcant?" Magnus asked.

"Achaius estimates a two month campaign ending in stalemate, unless we receive reinforcements," Marcant said.

"By the Five! So much for asking for his support," Telisa said to Magnus privately.

"But that analysis does not take the Trilisk AI into account," Marcant added quickly.

"Okay. We'll get it working." Magnus dropped the connection.

Telisa started to pace.

"This is so frustrating! We've come all this way with this huge fleet, and now the AI stops working? Why can't anything just be easy?"

"Sometimes it's easy, sometimes not. You don't remember the times it's easy."

"Not helpful. We're on the ropes. Time for a creative move," Telisa said.

Magnus smiled. "No shortcuts. We can start by testing one of the theories about the AI malfunction. If we can eliminate a possibility, it'll be a step in the right direction."

"Yes? Let's try it out."

Telisa's voice sounded hopeful.

Magnus opened a channel to Lieutenant Barrai and added Telisa in.

"Lieutenant. Anomaly report," Magnus ordered.

"Nothing new yet today," Barrai responded within a couple of seconds. "Though the anomalies I've already reported seem quite significant to me."

The tone of her voice expressed that she had noted Telisa's lack of concern with the anomalies seen thus far. Various ship's systems operated at higher efficiency than they should, and minor incidents that should have caused damage had not needed any repair.

"We have a special exercise for you today," Magnus said. "I want you to go on battle alert and charge all the power rings to maximum capacity. Then monitor the power levels and report anything unusual to us."

"Look for more anomalies," Barrai summarized. She spoke professionally, but submerged in her voice was a tiny sliver of... what? Suspicion? Amusement? Hope?

She knows that we're doing things that cause anomalies. Though she doesn't know why. Maybe she thinks we do it on purpose to test her. I should be as upfront as I can.

"I suspect there will be anomalies," Magnus said. "Maybe hoping. It must be frustrating to be kept in the dark—"

"Part of my job, Team Member," Barrai said. "I'm accustomed to being informed only to my level. That's the Space Force."

Her voice had leveled out.

She's decided to be happy with whatever she can learn for herself from participating. Good. She'll be paying very, very close attention.

The ship informed him they were on battle alert as a drill.

Magnus flipped the sensors off in the cargo bay they had been using for the prayer experiments while the ship's massive power rings charged.

"Try to make some more war supplies now," Magnus suggested to Telisa.

"Let's leave this room. We can try from the bridge," Telisa said.

Magnus nodded. He had not yet come very close to the Trilisk robot. He resolved to avoid the hallway to the vault. He did not want the machine to teleport him a few light seconds out into the void.

They walked to the bridge and took very comfortable positions on the lounges. They waited for two more minutes as the ship's temporary power stores topped off. Then Magnus turned to Telisa.

"Try again."

"You think all that power will help? Worth a try," Telisa said excitedly.

"Actually I suspect that to the AI, it's not much power at all. But yes, worth trying."

Telisa closed her eyes and concentrated.

"Team Members!" Barrai practically yelled on the connection, even though the interface was mental.

"Report," Telisa said.

"Massive malfunction across all weapons systems! We've lost huge amounts of... TM, I don't know how the ship hasn't exploded. Shorts of this magnitude should have caused—"

"No shorts, Lieutenant. Stay calm. I know where the energy went."

"Yes, Team Member," Barrai said more calmly, though clearly exasperated.

Magnus activated the sensors in the bay. He accessed the video feed and saw four new missiles floating in the wide open space.

"Only four!" Telisa said, disappointed.

"Yes, but it was no coincidence that all that power drained. We're still onto something," Magnus said. "And we made more than before."

"It needs energy. Lots of it," Telisa said. "Maybe it really will get more powerful if we move toward the star."

"Maybe."

"Then we head in there and hope it works. The Five help us if it doesn't have any effect."

Chapter 8

Caden could tell by the look on Siobhan's face when she walked into his quarters that she had steeled herself for some serious talk. The normal Siobhan was carefree and eager to share some plan for fun, but now she moved slowly and her face was a tight mask. He stood up from his chair.

"I promise you have nothing to worry about with me and Arakaki," Caden said emphatically.

"It's not that," Siobhan said. She looked pained.

Is she going to preemptively break up with me just to make her disaster scenario impossible?

"What's wrong?"

"Back on Earth... the first time we came back as PIT members..." Siobhan started slowly.

"Yes," he said patiently.

"I had to get my revenge on Spero. I was desperate, Caden. I *had* to load the dice in my favor."

"Right. So what happened?"

"Shiny helped me. He set me up with some serious Vovokan firepower."

"Wow. You never mentioned that before."

"I was foolish. Focused on that one goal. I agreed to do something for Shiny in return."

"Ohhhh no..."

"I had to succeed. I didn't have any thoughts of 'later'."

"Okay. I understand," Caden said calmly. "What does he want from you now?"

Siobhan glanced around as if afraid of being overheard.

"He wants me to *keep the war from ending*," she hissed.

"What!? How?"

"He says I should do whatever it takes. He wants this system destroyed!"

Caden realized his look of amazement probably was not helping. He turned aside and started to think aloud.

"At least they *are* our enemies... I don't feel bad for the Quarus. They came after the most peaceful race we've met... still, we can't betray the team like this. We can't work behind their back with Shiny!"

"I know! But... Caden, where I come from, you don't back out of a deal," she said.

I have to shut this down hard!

Caden spread his arms wide.

"He's an alien tyrant. You can't let millions die over this!" he said loudly. "This is Mr. Instant Betrayal we're talking about. He would never live up to his end if it were inconvenient for *him*."

"Okay. Yes. But Shiny said he would go competitive over it. What if it's about our life or death?"

"Telisa needs to know about this. We have to figure a way out together."

"What will she do? What will we do? This threatens the whole team."

"Telisa has been fighting against Shiny for a while now," Caden said. "I bet she deals with threats like this from him all the time and she's been shielding us from it."

Siobhan leaned forward and rested her head against his.

"I couldn't take it. I had to tell you. But I'm afraid to tell her."

"You haven't done anything wrong. As long as we tell her now."

Siobhan nodded.

"Okay, that's my opinion. You decide. I'll back you, whatever you want," he said.

Siobhan embraced him.

"I have decided. You're right; I just need help doing it, that's all."

Siobhan was the bravest person he had ever met. Considering the company he kept, that was significant. Now she looked fearful. It was not the personal danger they faced, it was the possibility of letting down the team.

"Telisa will know what to do," he reiterated. "And she won't blame you. Shiny used Magnus against her, remember?"

They stood together.

"She knows we're coming," Siobhan said. She walked to the door.

"The problem won't be with Telisa finding out about this," Caden told her as they headed for Telisa's quarters. "The hard part will be deciding if we're going to do what he wants."

"How could we keep a war going for him? More sentient beings will die."

"Well for starters we might not have a choice. The Quarus might keep fighting anyway. Then we can spin it to Shiny that you pulled it off for him."

Caden did not quite buy his own positive narrative. Telisa planned to spare the Quarus planets if she could. That would not work with Shiny's demand.

They came to the last hallway and paused at Telisa's closed door. Siobhan was in link contact with Telisa, so the door opened momentarily.

They walked in. Telisa looked them over for a moment. They had her full attention.

"Something come up with your Celaran investigations? Or the plans to use the AI for factories in the belt?"

"I have bad news," Siobhan said. She looked down at the floor. Her head actually hung. Caden stood straight. He squeezed her hand.

Telisa noticed Siobhan's distress and focused on her.

"Let me know what's up, and we'll deal with it."
Siobhan swallowed.

"Turns out I owe Shiny a favor from before the revolution at Sol. He's called in his marker and told me to make sure we don't make peace with the Quarus!"

Telisa looked surprised, but she handled it well.

"Thanks for telling me," Telisa said. Her voice was level. "I won't forget your loyalty."

"You don't seem as upset as I thought you would be," Siobhan said.

"Well I know Shiny's a snake, and your bad news is mixing with good right now," Telisa said. "We've discovered what's holding the AI back."

"What is it?" Siobhan asked.

"Power. It clearly needs more," Telisa said. "We charged up the rings for *Sharplight*'s high-energy weapons array, and the AI sucked that energy up in a millisecond."

"We never had a problem like that before," Caden said. "Was it ever really drawing crazy power from the other ships or the asteroid base?"

"Not that I was ever aware of. Shiny would have been aware of it for sure... it might be that this AI is missing its primary power source, but it has backup methods."

"What are we going to do?" Siobhan asked, still distraught.

"We're going to brainstorm about it at the next team meeting. Don't worry. This is why we have a bright and diverse team. We'll come up with a plan. We'll resist him together."

Chapter 9

Marcant opened a connection to Telisa with Adair and Achaius on the channel.

"We're getting ready to deploy the Trilisk detection network Aiye brought," Marcant said. "We've found a blocker."

"What's the problem?"

"Once Aiye deploys its hardware, the *Sharplight* is going to be first and foremost on the detection results," Adair said. "The dilemma that faces us is: how to keep Aiye from finding out about the Trilisk AI?"

"This has been coming up a lot lately," Telisa said.

"Really?"

"In different contexts, yes. But the bottom line is looking more and more like if we want to really use our Trilisk AI to its full potential, then Shiny is going to find out about it. If we try to be subtle, it might not tip the balance in our favor."

"I suggest we tell Aiye we have Trilisk toys that will show up on the scans," Achaius said. "Further: let Aiye scan Telisa and convince itself that she's not occupied by a Trilisk."

Telisa sighed.

"Yes. We need that system-wide detection. I'm just worried that Aiye's report of our Trilisk toys will make it clear to Shiny that we have an AI."

"I suspect that depends on how we use the AI," Achaius said. "If the whole fleet can clearly see its effects, then Shiny will likely figure it out."

"Subtle would be better. I'll keep that in mind," Telisa said.

"She is *not* a happy Citizen," Adair said privately to Marcant and Achaius.

"Yes. She's in some kind of crisis," Achaius agreed.

"Aiye is technically Space Force," Marcant said to Telisa. "Do you have reason to believe that Aiye's real loyalty is to Shiny?"

"No. I'm assuming this secret is too big to keep for long," Telisa said.

"You could ask Sager about Aiye before proceeding, if you trust him," Achaius said. "I get the feeling he's an unwilling Vovokan vassal."

"Sager is smart enough to walk a line between Shiny and us without letting either side know who he's really loyal to," Telisa said. "Besides, if I were Shiny, I would have hacked Sager's link a long time ago."

"I agree Shiny must have methods of watching the Space Force, and maybe even us," Adair said. "But it's probably not the link. Sager will be checking the integrity of his link as often as we double check our own links."

"Not helpful," Marcant said.

"I'll have Sager over for an FTF before I speak with Aiye," Telisa said. "Thanks for pointing out the issue and your suggestions."

***

Five hours after the talk with Telisa, Marcant was surprised to receive a request to attend an FTF with Telisa, Sager, and Aiye scheduled for the end of the shift.

I guess the accelerated schedule should not surprise me. This is critical. She can't wait long.

Even so, Marcant had not expected to be part of any such meeting. Had she invited him because he had brought his concerns to her, or had he moved up in the local hierarchy?

The only thing I know for sure is that Telisa is at the top of the PIT team and Magnus is not far below her. He shrugged. *Politics.*

He sauntered into the assigned room on a restricted deck of the *Sharplight*. The center of the room held a fountain instead of a table, and the air smelled of a mossy forest. The illusion ended there, though, as the walls were dark green instead of a forest scene.

"Welcome," Telisa said to him.

"Hi," he responded, finding a low stone seat. Sager walked in a few moments later.

"Admiral Sager. Thank you for joining us."

"I'm curious to hear what you wanted to meet in person about," Sager said. He settled onto one of the squat seats.

"It's about Aiye and its Trilisk detection network."

"I'm intrigued. Is this a test run of the detection system?"

"In a way, yes. First, may I ask you, is Aiye loyal to the Space Force?"

Sager did a double-take. He considered his answer, then responded confidently.

"Absolutely. We're all devoted to protecting Sol from another takeover."

"But Shiny is at the top of the control hierarchy, yes? Is Aiye the kind of rigid disciplinarian that sees Shiny's word as the ultimate law?"

Sager took a deep breath.

"I think I get what you're aiming at," Sager said. "Aiye is intelligent and perceptive. I suspect that Aiye understands the gray area involved in having multiple loyalties. Aiye is not under Shiny's direct control as far as I know. On the other hand, Aiye, like many of us, are appreciative of what Shiny has done *so far*."

"Snuzzle hashes! He's hinting that he likes Shiny too, more or less," Marcant said to Telisa privately.

"He's just saying he's withholding full trust in Shiny, but he doesn't want to preemptively betray the Vovokan," Telisa said.

"Really? You got all that? You're better at this than I am."

Telisa continued aloud.

"Shiny sends us out to find alien tech for him. We bring that back to him. However, at our discretion, we are allowed to keep some of the artifacts for ourselves to make us more effective in the field. Aiye's scans will likely reveal that."

Sager absorbed her summary for a moment.

"I understand. You have some tricks up your sleeve for this offensive, as you've hinted at."

"Yes. Trilisk tricks. I'm just trying to give you and Aiye the heads up that we're using this kind of technology before Aiye activates the network and sees that for itself. I want to prevent a sequence of events where Aiye tells you we've got a Trilisk here on the *Sharplight* in the middle of a battle and you have to figure out what to do about it."

Sager nodded, but he looked a little puzzled.

"He wonders why you brought him here incarnate to say all this," Marcant said privately.

"I agree," Telisa replied to Marcant.

"We may as well let Aiye join us now," Telisa said. Sager nodded.

The silver android entered the room fifteen seconds later. It sat squarely on one of the chairs even though it clearly did not need to, probably to make the Terrans feel more comfortable.

I'm glad Achaius and Adair don't want bodies like that.

"What is the objective of our meeting?" Aiye asked.

"I'll answer that in a roundabout way... Aiye, we welcome your help to check the system for Trilisks. I suspect you'll find some. However, I need to set expectations about what you'll likely see."

"You have intel on Trilisks in the system?" Aiye asked.

"Kind of. I'm a Trilisk host body, though I'm not controlled by a Trilisk," Telisa said. "I wanted to give you the opportunity to get in whatever scans you need now to help convince you of that."

"I appreciate that," Aiye said. "I have precious few scans of the host bodies, and this should help. However, I don't think this would come up as an alarm in my system scans. I don't think the host bodies give off the same types of energy that we're looking for."

"Good. However, we have Trilisk technology in play as well. Because of that, I think the *Sharplight* will show up in your scans. I wanted to tell you that up front, and to give you a chance to see that baseline now, before the combat begins."

"I see. You're trying to prevent an incident in response to what I'll see from the *Sharplight*," Aiye said.

"Yes. I want to cooperate with you in vetting the crew and making sure we're not under Trilisk control."

"Very well. The detection devices we've brought are already on their way to points throughout the system, but we have many spares. I'll set those up locally and start monitoring the *Sharplight* right away."

"Good. Thank you," Telisa said.

"Will I be allowed to examine the decks that have been off-limits to non-PIT members?"

"No, I can't do that."

"Yet you predict there will be Trilisk signs from the *Sharplight*. What is to stop me from concluding that if it looks like a duck, swims like a duck, and quacks like a duck, then it probably is a duck?"

Marcant frowned.

What did it just say?

Telisa appeared confused as well.

"I don't follow you," she said. "I have a feeling Maxsym might know what you're talking about."

"If I detect Trilisk emanations here, but I can't look for one, then why wouldn't I conclude there is a Trilisk on one of the restricted decks?"

"Oops," Marcant said to Telisa privately.

"We have to let Aiye search the whole ship," she replied.

"You understand that if there is a Trilisk aboard, and it has enslaved all of us, when you go looking for it, it will simply take you over as well," Telisa said to the group.

"That's a possibility, but if we assume we are helpless before all Trilisks, why are we even trying? Why build a detection network at all?" asked Aiye.

"We could do it to avoid them. To steer clear," Sager said.

"Or one Trilisk could be in conflict with others," Aiye said.

Telisa sighed.

"Okay, I'll allow you to access the restricted decks," she said. "I'm trying to stay low key and escape notice. I'd appreciate it if all this could stay between us. I don't want the entire Space Force to know about this."

"So that if I do discover a Trilisk and I must be eliminated, no one will be informed enough to worry?"

"You work with a team? You could tell them," Telisa said, exasperated.

"I already have," Aiye said. "I think this was a very productive meeting. We should be ready to move ahead very soon."

Marcant felt a headache coming on.

Chapter 10

Magnus embraced Telisa on the warm floor of her room. The sleep web dangled above, free of their weight after they accidentally fell from it half an hour ago.

She sighed. Magnus watched her face; he could see her mind turn back to serious matters.

"We have so many big decisions to make, and they have to be made... now," Telisa said.

"About how to power the Trilisk AI?" Magnus asked.

"We need to power the AI, placate Shiny if we manage to end the war, keep him from finding out our secret, or deal with him if he does find out. The problems are stacking up faster than we can find solutions."

"Let's get all the brains working on these problems, not just ours," Magnus said. "We can meet—"

"All we do is meet and talk. We need to *take action*!" Telisa said, venting some frustration.

"When we have a workable plan, we will," Magnus said soothingly.

Telisa turned away in the dim light. Magnus recognized that she was processing link traffic. He waited.

"It's Barrai again. No doubt she has another anomaly to report," Telisa said.

Magnus nodded. Telisa added him to the channel.

"Hello, Lieutenant."

"Another anomaly to report," Barrai said.

"Yes?" Telisa replied.

"The ship is missing six percent of its mass," Barrai said, deadpan.

"What?"

"The ship is missing six percent of its mass, Team Member. I have identified the areas where the mass is missing, excepting only those areas of the ship I am not allowed to enter or scan, and I'm ready to give a detailed report."

"Thank you for bringing this to my attention. Well done. Are we in imminent danger of structural or systems failures?"

"No. The ship *is* weaker, but the mass has been taken from clever places and in conservative amounts. Quite ingenious, actually, though I can't figure out—"

"Stand by, Lieutenant," Telisa said, cutting the connection.

"Are you thinking what I'm thinking?" Magnus asked.

"The AI used that mass to make the missiles," Telisa said excitedly.

"Yes. And perhaps more than that," Magnus said. "It needs power, too, remember? What if it annihilated some of that mass to power the entire procedure?"

"Mass to energy conversion? Or even both directions... and when we used the other AIs—"

"They had mass available. Either from a planet, or asteroids, or whatever. Out here on the edges of this star system, it only has these ships to work with. Maybe even just *this* ship."

"Lieutenant," Telisa said, returning to the other channel. "Send a pointer to Marcant. Your discovery here is vital. Again, well done."

Telisa rolled away and dressed as she switched to the team channel.

"Marcant. The AI needs mass to work with. It's been cannibalizing the ship," she said.

"Mass? By the Purple Paste Nebula, that makes sense for a Trilisk machine. It gets whatever it needs to operate from the environment. So advanced it doesn't need specialized materials or... power sources. It can probably convert mass to energy too, to power itself!"

"We think so, yes. If we can get to the asteroid belt, we should have plenty of material for it to use. I'll have a pointer sent over to you."

Magnus felt the same satisfaction at the news that Telisa obviously did. If they could get the Trilisk AI ball rolling again, it could unlock the way to solving their other problems.

We need material, but we're too far out, and we can't go farther into the system without a big fight.... but there is material out here... if you know where to look.

Magnus double checked the shared system map and found what he needed. He asked the *Sharplight*'s navigation services to get him some solutions.

"Telisa. There are two large comets we could intercept on the way in," Magnus said. "It would be costly in terms of our own energy, but if the AI can use that mass, it'll bring us ahead. There's also a dark planetoid beyond the nearest gas giant, though it's less conveniently placed and possibly too large to divert."

"Sounds promising," she said.

Telisa turned the lights on in her quarters. Magnus checked the results of his quick navigation requests as he dressed. They showed intercept courses and acceleration plans for the comets that brought them to the same destination near the belt. He sent pointers along to Telisa.

She paused to review his findings.

"Do it. If we're right—and I think we are—this will be exactly what it needs. I can produce missiles, kinetic pellets, even increase the energy weapons output of the ship. Anything we can think of."

"You might want to pray for the missing mass to be replaced at some point as well," Magnus said. The thought of heading into a system-wide space battle was daunting enough—much more so knowing part of the ship's structure was missing.

"Will do. Send that information to Sager so he can pull a couple of ships and get us that mass. Tell him we accelerate for the belt within the hour."

Michael McCloskey

"We don't actually know this will work," Magnus warned.

"We're out of time," Telisa said. "Our allies will, for the time being, still attack the belt. If we can't get the AI working then that will have to be enough."

"Team, this is it," Telisa transmitted to the team channel. "I won't delay any longer. We think we know what the Trilisk AI needs, but we might be wrong. In any case, stay sharp. If everything goes according to plan, we'll have very little to do except watch the battle play out, but you never know what might happen."

Magnus knew that was true enough. He wondered what his personal odds of surviving the fight would be. The simulations said they had an 80% chance of victory in the battle for the outer system alone, comprising only the gas giant moon bases and the asteroid belt factories, but usually at a cost great enough that hitting the inner system next would be a toss-up.

The attack had been run in a thousand simulations already: the main plan called for the fleet to head directly for a short segment of the belt where a massive fortress had been detected. It was expected that the massive combined firepower of the fleet would obliterate the fortress in short order. From there, the Celarans would attack spinward and the Terrans in the opposite direction. The fleets would attack along the ring of asteroids, moving at sublight velocity relative to the belt, concentrating their firepower on small parts of the ring at a time. The Terran fleet was larger, and thus had a much more aggressive attack schedule that would bring them over 70% of the belt in the time the Celarans would cover 30% of it. Once there, the fleet would be reunited and ready to either attack the inner system or disengage.

One great flaw of the preparations that Magnus regretted was that it did not include the use of the AI. Between wanting to hide the AI as much as possible and not even knowing if it would work at all, they had to plan the attack as if it did not exist. The best Magnus had been able to do was stress to Sager the importance of a flexible attack schedule, which he had sold on the basis of varying resistance from the enemy. If the AI came back to life and they were able to obliterate their enemies easily, then the attack schedule would change to take advantage of that.

The fleet had a million targets in the belt. The critical targets had been assigned to ships (sometimes more than one) in an order of incidence. Other points of interest in the belt were left as targets of opportunity.

Magnus watched the fleet move out on the shared map in his PV. The various squadrons lined up for the belt with the light elements in the lead. He headed for the bridge with Telisa to watch the battle unfold.

Michael McCloskey

Chapter 11

The pieces were coming together for the attack. Telisa noted that the first comet had been brought within 100,000 kilometers of the *Sharplight* to feed the AI. Meanwhile, the lead elements of the fleet reached a point which marked the release of the first salvo on the asteroid fortress and its surrounding space factories. The *Sharplight* had attained its attack velocity relative to the target.

Telisa started a countdown timer as the fleet map lit up with thousands of missiles. The big ships began their energy weapon assault at the same moment as the launch, and the timer would help her calculate when they would see the results from their position many light-minutes out from the targets. Since their sensors in the system did not have tachyon emitters to talk to the fleet's TRB, she would have to wait for the light from the base's destruction to reach them. The beams would strike in minutes, and minutes more after that, everyone could see the results. With luck, the beams would inflict enough damage to compromise the missile defenses and doom the defenders.

Magnus, Caden, and Siobhan monitored the action with her from the armored bridge lounge of the *Sharplight*. Barrai worked from the secondary bridge closer to the ship's weapons.

Telisa dropped the point-blank sensor array, then closed her eyes and thought of a vast field of tungsten pellets in formation with the *Sharplight*. After a half minute, she reactivated the sensors in the area and looked at the results in her PV.

"Still nothing. I'll try again when it's within 75,000 kilometers," she said.

The PIT team focused on the battle data in their personal views. To wait even minutes seemed agony. Telisa grimly accepted that if death came in the coming days, it might well be instantaneous and they might never know what hit the *Sharplight*.

The timer reached zero. Telisa zoomed her system map to focus on the belt at the point of their attacks. Red and yellow blossomed across her viewpane.

"It looks good," Caden said. "That superfortress has been atomized!"

The automated analyses reaffirmed his words: all targets destroyed.

"So far, so good," she said.

This was the easiest part. With the fleets relatively clumped up, they enjoyed a significant concentration of firepower.

Telisa had the routine automated by the time her next attempt came due. The sensors dropped, and she concentrated for a half minute. The settings returned to normal. Her heart leaped with excitement when she saw a vast field of tiny, dense masses out in space. The masses were motionless relative to the *Sharplight*, which meant they were traveling at a large fraction of lightspeed toward the Quarus belt defenses.

"Kinetic weapons deployed," Telisa announced. "Lieutenant Barrai, shape our spinner field to aim them at a target near the front of our queue that's unlikely to be able to avoid the attack."

"Aye, Team Member!" Barrai said.

The *Sharplight* nudged forward, putting the pellets into an asymmetric zone of its spinner field. The pellets accelerated away toward a target in the belt ahead: a Quarus mining base.

Minutes later, the belt exploded with light. The Terran missile wave had arrived well after the first energy strikes, pulverizing the smaller Quarus bases around the fortress. The shared map showed dozens more destroyed targets.

"This is within our more optimistic simulation ranges," Marcant said from elsewhere on the ship.

"Achaius and I are adjusting our simulation constants to match observed results."

Up until now, everything had been an educated guess—how many of the incoming missiles could the Quarus hit and with what accuracy? How effective were their energy and kinetic point defenses and electronic countermeasures? How maneuverable were the asteroid bases? Future simulations would have greater accuracy.

"Their asteroid bases can rotate to place assets on the far side from us, but no appreciable number of those rocks are actually able to accelerate to avoid incoming salvoes," Magnus noted.

Telisa created another field of tungsten pellets in formation with the vessel.

"Launch this batch, I need to check something else," Telisa told Magnus and Barrai.

"How are those being deployed?" Barrai asked. "It's like they just show up on the sensors periodically. I can see TMs Magnus and Telisa manipulating the sensor settings, but... those are real, aren't they?"

"Deadly real," Magnus assured her.

Barrai launched the next field of pellets at the enemy.

Telisa felt nerves clenching her gut.

The AI is helping, but I'm not thinking big enough. It's capable of more, I'm sure. A Trilisk would know what to do.

This was one of the possible turning points in the many simulations they had run. The entire belt crawled with the Quarus, their ships, and their machines. Now that the attacking fleets had revealed themselves, the entire ring was alerted. If the Quarus launched missiles at the fleet, starting with the farthest reaches of the ring, with each point firing with a delay such that every missile in the entire ring reached the fleet at the same time, their defenses would be overwhelmed. The combined fleet losses could be as high as thirty percent in one salvo.

Telisa saw evidence of a variant of that strategy rolling out. Missiles were launching in a growing wave, starting from almost a hundred million kilometers out. Each military ship and station added to its own ordnance to the wave as it passed, rapidly growing the number of missiles in flight. It was not the entire asteroid ring, but it was still a huge counterattack.

"Well, we knew this would happen," Magnus said grimly. "Now we get to find out if we're as good at stopping those missiles as we hope we are."

"If we're still alive afterward, I look forward to updating the simulations again," Marcant quipped.

Telisa watched the numbers grow on a viewpane in her mind.

"I have an idea," she said. "It's hard to pray up useful things because I have to know all the designs and get every detail perfect, but what if I wanted to break something?"

"I see what you mean," Siobhan said. "You probably don't need to know how those incoming missiles work to, say, turn their cases into jelly."

"Should we give the AI away so soon? The campaign just started," Caden said.

"Given how much trouble we've had with it, we don't dare wait longer, since it might not work," Marcant said.

"Valid points. I want to be using it for something now, though, to reduce our losses," Telisa said. "Close battles will snowball one way or the other, so an edge at the start is huge."

"That's exactly what Achaius said," Marcant commented.

"A hybrid approach might be good," Magnus said. "Wait and hit the incoming wave *after* it's come through our outer layer of missile defense. That way, you still protect us, but we can learn how effective our conventional defenses are. It will also be less apparent that we 'cheated' with some superweapon."

"There are real Space Force ships out there!" Telisa protested.

"Anything of ours out that far is a robotic ship," Magnus explained. He shared a view of the Terran fleet with several perimeter lines demarcated. Telisa saw the distance Magnus referred to.

"Let's do it," Telisa agreed.

The Terran fleet initiated a course change as it approached the asteroids to traverse the rest of the belt counter-spinward. The Celarans faced their own wall of incoming ordnance to spinward. At least the Celaran ships were better at evasion and cloaking, so they might be able to avoid a portion of the counter-launch. Telisa would focus only on her own arm of the assault.

The team fidgeted and watched the map as the weapons closed. It was all too easy to think of the whole thing as another distant simulation unrelated to reality. It seemed an eternity until the wave reached the first extents of the Terran fleet.

The robot frigates in its path released their point defenses. Telisa watched as many of the incoming objects were destroyed, but the wave overwhelmed the ships. The front line became red dots of light on the shared map as the retaliatory missile wave destroyed them. Telisa watched a feed from one such ship. One moment it soared majestically through the void, the next it burned brightly, then finally its cooling fragments dispersed in the emptiness.

Feelings of panic tried to rise in Telisa, but she forced herself to calm. She had mastered this kind of fear long ago when she faced danger with Magnus on a far away alien world.

Telisa imagined the incoming missiles, flying through space, closing on the Terran ships. Then she imagined an invisible wave coming out to meet them. When the wave hit the missiles, it dashed them aside, smashing them each into tiny pieces.

"Nothing's happening!" Caden said.

"Patience," Magnus said.

Telisa ignored them and kept working. She started from the beginning again. The invisible wave pulsed outward, toward the incoming threats. Then it struck them, obliterating each missile.

"There! It's working! Keep going!" Magnus urged.

Telisa concentrated longer. She watched the tiny dots on the map and willed the missiles to melt into goo and fly apart.

"Oh, wow!" Siobhan breathed.

"Yes!" Caden exulted simultaneously.

Telisa imagined some of the missiles running into others and detonating.

"That's it! You did it!" Caden said.

Telisa opened her eyes and smiled.

"Now we have the advantage."

"It was impressive. The missiles died off in three distinct events," Marcant said.

"Which one was most effective? I was trying for different things."

"The second was better than the first. But I can't compare it to the third, because there were only a few left at that point. We don't really know how many that last one could have taken out."

"We might want to fundamentally change our strategy. Keep the fleet more tightly packed so it can operate under the protection of the AI," Magnus said.

"The manned ships, maybe," Telisa said.

"Clustering the fleet too much might pose other dangers," Marcant countered.

Telisa closed her eyes and envisioned more occurrences.

"What are you doing?" Siobhan asked.

"We might be thinking too small," Telisa said. "I'm going to try and pray one of those asteroid fortresses away."

"Worth a try! The battle could be over before it even started," Magnus said.

Telisa muted her channels and concentrated on a huge Quarus base in the shared system map. It was a powerful military station built into a massive asteroid.

Destroy that base. Atomize it. Boom. I need that base destroyed.

Telisa concentrated on it for a couple of minutes. Then she returned her attention to the shared system map and waited for the light from the base's destruction to reach them. It would be several minutes before she would know if it worked.

Telisa created another batch of pellets, and then another. Each time, Barrai used the ship's spinner to accelerate the tiny projectiles toward the target.

The time came and went. The system map did not show anything of note in the vicinity of the fortress she had targeted.

"The Five in slumber," she said. "No effect on that base."

"Well, we've sent out several kinetic pellet salvoes, why don't you start taking out targets with the heavy energy weapon?" Magnus suggested.

"Absolutely. I'm going to add Barrai and you all to a new channel," Telisa said aloud. "She needs to be on the same page. Try not to mention Trilisks or anything too specific."

Telisa called the new channel the crew channel. Barrai joined it quickly.

"Lieutenant Barrai. You're free to fire. Here's our final list of targets for the energy weapons," Telisa said, sending a pointer to Barrai.

"Yes ma'am. That's a long list. We have days worth of targets there," she noted.

"Not necessarily," Telisa said enigmatically. "Let's see how it goes. Fire at will, Lieutenant."

Barrai did not comment. The ship's energy rings started to charge.

"Achaius, we need you. Please use our special equipment to boost the damage output of the *Sharplight*."

"Achaius is going to... take the lead now?" Magnus asked.

"Achaius understands the physics of the *Sharplight*'s high energy weaponry. Increasing the power of those weapons is far more complicated than making kinetic pellets. Whatever can be done to bolster it, I think it'll be able to do it better."

Probably much better.

Barrai ran the energy in the ship's rings through the Sharplight's energy weapons. The entire procedure was immensely complex, but the sophistication of the timings and EM flow manipulation was hidden from her, controlled by the computers. The energy in the power rings dropped to zero as the ship discharged a full strike.

"Team Member! The output is... it's simply impossible," Barrai said.

"We're using alien technology to boost your power," Telisa told her. Telisa looked at the readings. The *Sharplight* had just emitted a single blast twelve times more powerful than it should have been capable of.

"That should be enough for the first target, yes? Move on to the next. Cycle through our targets as they come in range. Use the shared targets of opportunity to fill in the rest of the time. I'll ask Sager to provide more for us."

"Yes, TM," Barrai breathed. She was clearly still grappling with what had happened.

Telisa opened a connection to Admiral Sager.

"Admiral. I need to coordinate with you to accelerate the *Sharplight*'s attack schedule," she said.

"Of course. You'll need a lot more targets with that kind of firepower," Sager said excitedly.

"Oh, you noticed?"

"My electromagnetic warfare officers are mesmerized. One of them said that's not even the *Sharplight*. She demanded to know what you had done with the real ship. The fleet's high energy weapons people want what you've got over there, TM."

"Then send over the six biggest battleships you've got, and I'll give it to them," Telisa said. "Please tell your officers it's the benefits of a special TM dreadnought."

"What about... hiding the AI?" Magnus asked off channel.

"We're going to win this fight, even if we have to show Shiny what we've got," Telisa said.

"You're serious? I'll send them toward you immediately. How close to you?" asked Sager.

"Let's try a hexagon formation around *Sharplight* at... 30,000 kilometers," Telisa said.

If this thing is designed to work across a variety of planets, that should be within its range.

"I'm reconfiguring part of the fleet to screen you from counterattack," Sager said. "If you can do for those ships what you have working on *Sharplight*, we won't need those lighter elements hitting the belt facilities."

The fleet began to reconfigure as Sager sent orders and worked out the details.

"This would have been better if we had known we would get it working again and had no secrets from the fleet," Magnus told her on a private channel.

"Yes, if it had baked into the plan from the start, that would have been nice. But this is where we find ourselves," she said.

"Achaius? How are our comets holding up?" Telisa asked on the team channel, knowing Barrai would not hear.

"I speak in place of Achaius," Adair replied. "Achaius is too busy praying... never thought I would say that... you still have 91% of the mass left. There's a huge amount of energy here, though I don't know how efficient the Trilisk device is at converting it. By the time we burn through it, we should be close enough to use the asteroids."

"I'd like to know exactly how close the source material needs to be, but the middle of a battle is probably not the best time to find out."

"I don't think we'll have to do anything except observe. If the AI can draw power from the asteroids, I assume it will."

The battleships came into the new configuration one by one, each at the point of a hexagon perpendicular to *Sharplight*'s course. Telisa waited until they were all in place and contacted Adair again.

"Ask Achaius if he can do this for those battleships in our new formation," Telisa said.

Telisa checked sensor data in a PV. The numbers jumped as the battleships began to fire.

"Frackjammers!" Siobhan exclaimed.

"By the Five," Telisa said, looking at an external feed of the fleet. The *Sharplight* and its surrounding battleships were dishing out more energy than the combined fleet had been able to output in the initial attack on the asteroid fortress.

Okay, so we've shown our hand. The Quarus will see we have something they can't match, though the Space Force people will see it, too.

Minutes later the full analyses of the devastation poured in. The augmented energy weapons were vaporizing everything in their path. The Quarus were managing to bend some of the incoming beams slightly off target by means unknown, but it was not enough. The ships blasted through their queue of targets at increased rates of fire. Achaius was doing more than just increasing the power of the beams; he was also keeping the battleships' energy rings perpetually full so that the assault group could process targets in their queues as fast as they could bring them up and fire.

"This is a game changer," Sager said incredulously. "We need to press this advantage hard while we can. The campaign could be over in days instead of weeks."

Another wave of missiles launched at the fleet, but it was smaller than the first retaliation. Many of the Quarus bases had already been hit. The Terran fleet pressed through the reduced resistance with minimal losses.

They settled into a rhythm of targeting and destroying batches of targets. As the first shift passed, the resistance became sporadic, and therefore much less dangerous. The smaller ships stopped all threats to the special PIT weapons formation with their own point defense weapons. The Terran fleet worked its way around the ring of rocks orbiting the star ahead of schedule.

As they approached the end of the Terran portion of the belt, well into the second shift of the offensive, Telisa prepared to move beyond it. The team would need to sleep soon, but for the moment they were buoyed by the adrenaline of their victories.

"Coordinate with the Celaran fleet and get us an extended list of targets from their area of the belt," Telisa ordered.

"Aye aye," the admiral responded.

Within seconds the *Sharplight*'s target list expanded.

"You'll see new targets in our queue. They're in the Celaran section of the belt, nevertheless, proceed with the strikes including these new ones," Telisa told Barrai.

Barrai sent a nonverbal ack.

Telisa wondered what they had left in their wake. She saw over a hundred small ships on the shared campaign map heading toward the inner system. The Space Force had marked them as escape pods and small ships fleeing the assault. The fleet would not fire at them.

Are they terrified? Angry? Planning to regroup and return?

Small squads of three to seven ships had been stationed here and there in the belt to evaluate the damage done to the enemy and scout for problems. She did not know how the Quarus refugees might react. If they prepared to join a counterattack from the inner system, she wanted to know about it.

"In another five minutes. there won't be any major threats left in the belt," Magnus said. "The power Achaius and the AI have achieved was overkill for those targets. We obliterated the asteroids we had targeted. In fact, the Quarus will have to use their defense satellites to screen their planets from the waves of rock which will be raining into the inner system for years to come."

The Terran fleet changed its formation toward the inner system.

"Forming back up with the Celaran fleet. They've lost a few ships," Sager noted. Telisa watched the map as the fleets started to reorganize. It looked like it would take hours.

"It's eerie to sit and watch the action from a screen, as if it isn't real," Caden said.

"I was thinking the same thing. It's too easy to wage a war this way," Siobhan added.

Too easy. Yes. We killed thousands of Quarus and destroyed a huge industrial base that must have taken a hundred years to build. And we just sat here and watched it happen in our PVs across the time of two or three shifts.

A data update from the inner system showed thousands of new objects in space.

"The Quarus are launching a counteroffensive from the inner system. It's the biggest ship action I've ever witnessed," Sager said. "And that includes a slew of simulations. I hope you've got plenty more firepower where that came from."

"We do! This was amazingly successful!" Barrai said. She did not seem to share the heavy mood of those in the main bridge.

"We'll have at least a day before they can bring their full force to bear out here," Magnus said.

"Well, hitting rocks is one thing," Telisa cautioned. "They weren't equipped to maneuver, so we could obliterate them from light minutes away. Not so with the Quarus home fleet."

"If the Quarus have the same weaknesses in space that they do planetside, I'd say we should put a lot of effort into producing more missiles and pellet fields," Magnus said.

"Good idea. We'll clean up the more predictably moving targets and switch over to a new plan to face their fleet."

Michael McCloskey

Chapter 12

Lieutenant Barrai sneaked a look at the system map even though she was off duty. She had put in a triple shift during the belt run, then grabbed a shift of sleep despite a Quarus counterattack launching from the inner system. She had expected to be back at the weapons as soon as she awakened, but as she slept it had become clear to the combined Celaran-Terran fleet that the Quarus were waging a campaign of attrition rather than launching a direct assault into the shattered belt.

The map displayed the fleets at a stand off well beyond reasonable energy weapons range. The Quarus were using stealthy weapons that slowly worked their way through the void and struck once they arrived at point blank range. The massive amount of debris caused by the destruction of the Quarus bases in the belt made threat detection much more difficult—billions of pieces of rock and metal were now flying around wreaking havoc with the Terran detection systems. Barrai felt that the leaders might take the fleets away from the belt any hour, giving up the cover that it offered in order to operate in a cleaner area.

She arrived at the gym where she had worked out with Maxsym and Marcant. Siobhan was already warming up, punching and kicking at her reflection in the mirrored wall.

"Hard to think about a workout with all that's going on, isn't it?" Siobhan said.

"A little. But the Space Force has trained me to understand that time off is as important as time on duty," Barrai said. Siobhan nodded.

I didn't sound very genuine. Just spouted some Space Force policy, Barrai thought.

Both women were already in fighting clothes: tough gi pants and rugged tops. Barrai noticed again how tall and lean Siobhan was. Her opponent looked supremely fit, and possessed a remarkable reach. Barrai estimated the challenge would be much greater today.

"Shall we do striking, rolling, or throwing? Or everything?" Barrai asked her.

"Everything. That's how it is in real life. Besides, you're challenging me today, right? Gonna find out where you are in the pecking order?" Siobhan said.

Direct girl. Very direct. She probably lassoed Caden and dragged him into her cave.

Barrai nodded.

"I guess that's more or less accurate," Barrai said.

She actually wanted long-term sparring partners, so direct competition might lead to unpleasantness that could ruin that. On the other hand, Siobhan was right: sometimes best to go hard with everything, even in an incarnate session or two, so they were prepared for the real world.

Barrai did forward rolls across the floor to a heavy bag which dropped from the ceiling. Then she tapped at it lightly to loosen up. After a few minutes of preparation, the two women faced each other at the center of the large room. The ceiling was high for a chamber on a spacecraft. The floor was softer than the metal, carbon, or ceramic decks elsewhere, but firm enough to keep their feet from sinking in.

She will attack first, Barrai thought.

Siobhan opened aggressively. She shot high and then dove low, going for Barrai's legs. Barrai simultaneously sprawled and jabbed Siobhan's face. Siobhan twisted to one side, pulling Barrai with her. They both hit the floor, still holding each other. Siobhan tried to control a leg, but Barrai threatened to respond with a heel kick from her other leg, so Siobhan disengaged.

The two regained their feet and circled each other. They traded strings of combinations for a minute, each one trying to put the other at a disadvantage. Barrai felt good:

her lungs worked hard, her heart pumped furiously, and sweat covered her skin. Siobhan smiled back at her like a maniac.

Barrai felt ready, so she stepped up the speed a notch. She whipped her right leg up and struck Siobhan's short ribs before her opponent could drop her elbow to cover them, then went for a head strike. Siobhan had taken the body hit, but she covered her head and even tried to catch Barrai's leg, but it was already withdrawn.

Barrai closed to jab hard, putting her weight into it. Siobhan took the jab square on the face. Barrai tried to deliver a hand combo off the initiative she had gained, but instead, she found herself flying through the air as Siobhan used Barrai's own forward charge to lead her into a throw. Barrai landed hard, not quite able to spread her impact or roll out of it gracefully.

Siobhan came in with a vengeance, trying to take a top mount and control her opponent. Barrai brought up her right leg behind Siobhan's left arm, then she slid her body out of the danger zone. The leg continued up and over Siobhan's shoulder, and now it was Siobhan who was in trouble with her left arm isolated. Barrai sat up as Siobhan planted into the floor face first. Siobhan tried to roll away, but Barrai wrapped the arm and leaned forward, putting pressure on the joint.

Siobhan tapped.

One for the good guys, Barrai thought. *Now she'll be trying to get me back.*

They stood and resumed. Barrai let Siobhan come in looking to redeem herself. Barrai let loose, hitting Siobhan more times.

Over the next few minutes, it became clear that despite the first submission, Barrai's advantage was actually in the standing game. She repeatedly hit Siobhan in the ribs and the face. Siobhan got in a good throw and one submission after that. Barrai decided they were about equal in a roll on the floor.

After another twenty minutes they took a break. They were each drenched and pulling in air hard.

Barrai decided now might be a good time to get some questions in. She could also try to gauge if she had ruffled Siobhan's feathers. She started with a compliment.

"The PIT team's capabilities have amazed me. I figured you wouldn't live up to the hype, but you've *exceeded* the abilities I imagined from everything I've heard."

"That's a weird thing to say after kicking my ass," Siobhan said.

"Oh! I was thinking of the display of firepower on the belt attack. I still can't believe the readings I got from *Sharplight*."

"Wonders would be a more normal occurrence if we embraced alien technology instead of squirreling it away from everyone," Siobhan said.

Anti-Space Force? Or just smarting from her loss?

"Thank you for the roughhousing," Barrai said sincerely.

Siobhan smiled. "Let's keep going. See if you have legs."

Barrai nodded. They went two more fifteen-minute rounds. Barrai did slow, but so did Siobhan, so they fought about even in the last round.

"Thanks for the workout," Siobhan said when they had finished. "I'm happy to get a new person with their own style on the rotation."

"You stole my line," Barrai said. "Thanks."

Barrai left for her quarters. As she cooled down, pain grew in her body. She felt her bruised ribs. Siobhan had gotten in some hard shots.

At this rate, I may never get to fight Telisa.

Despite the thought, the idea still excited her. What could she learn from the infamous leader of PIT? She would be an improved fighter and officer no matter what happened.

***

Maxsym pushed a hand through his short blond hair. His eyes felt sticky. He felt that if he looked in a mirror he would see dark rings under his eyes. He checked the time. He had already been working for two shifts on the project, punctuated by two more romps with Stracey.

The host body genome was radically more advanced than Terran, Celaran, or Quarus biology. It sucked up more computing resources to study for almost no results. Miss Stalos had served as a catalyst for understanding the Trilisk creations again, but now Maxsym was not so sure it was the right thing to be spending time on. On the other hand, he had no qualms about spending time on Stracey.

This is the work of a lifetime. Or two.

"I could have come up with useful results about the Quarus with this number of cycles," Maxsym said to himself, even though Stracey was just across the lab.

She heard him and replied out loud.

"It's hard to believe that the biology of living aliens can take second seat to anything, isn't it? But these host bodies are almost beyond understanding. Trilisk technology," Stracey said. She walked over to his station. "Still, we don't need to understand every nuance. I bet it's modularized. Eighty percent chance one of the areas we've marked is involved with remote control of the nervous system."

Maxsym could tell her passion for the science was real. She was not dissuaded by the magnitude of the task—quite the opposite.

"I think you've made real progress, but this is a career project. I could have produced some conclusions about the Quarus by now, something to help the war effort."

"I thought Telisa had approved."

"Yes, but does she understand what we're up against? She probably thinks we'll have the breakthrough in a month."

"Progress will snowball," Stracey insisted. "Besides... I'm having the time of my life, aren't you?"

They traded smiles. Still, Maxsym argued on.

"It takes orders of magnitude more computational power to analyze these elegant, multipurpose structures. I swear every fold of the proteins has ten different functions."

"But we have the tools here! These Vovokan machines are incredibly powerful! This ship might have as much number crunching power as the GNI setup back on Earth. Trying to get them to do anything... it's a completely different mindset. I know... they're alien machines, so what can I expect?"

Is this just how she is? Over the top enthusiasm all the time? It's like she's pressing for a sub-result she hasn't shared with me... but she's shared so much.

Maxsym received a connection request from Marcant.

"One moment. I have an incoming channel," Maxsym said. He turned away from her. "Marcant?"

"I've been meaning to ask you about breathing," Marcant said.

"Is this serious?"

"I've been undergoing a lot of physical training as you know, requirements of the team and all, and it came up. Should I be trying to control my breathing, strive to fill my lungs from the bottom, you know, using my diaphragm—"

"Well the answer is, it depends, of course," Maxsym said.

"On what?"

"On a million different things," Maxsym said. His exasperation came through in his voice a bit more than he wanted. "First of all, your rib muscles and your diaphragm are both part of the mechanics of all breathing, not just one or the other. Secondly, it depends on what you want to optimize. It also depends upon your own physique, genetics, blood characteristics, training... it goes on and on... don't you see?"

Maxsym found himself breathing hard.

What is this? Adrenal release? I'm not that angry...

"Well I can come up with some parameters for you," Marcant said after a moment. "Say I'm trying to optimize for hand-to-hand combat... Maxsym?"

I can't breathe!

Maxsym fell to his knees, gasping loudly.

"This isn't funny, Marcant!" he hissed. "Not..."

His own voice started to sound strange and his vision narrowed. Stracey said something as if from a great distance, but he could not make it out.

I'm blacking out, these are signs of...

Maxsym slipped away into the darkness.

***

Telisa awakened to an alert signal from her link. For once, she was alone in a sleep web with Magnus nowhere in sight.

She focused the alert in her PV. It was from the Vovokan *Iridar*: Team member down! Maxsym had suffered a serious mishap.

"By the Five! Maxsym!"

She hurriedly sifted through more of incoming data. Maxsym was alive, though barely, sustained by emergency services on the *Iridar*. Stracey Stalos had also been stricken, even worse.

"Stracey Stalos is dead!" she said on the PIT channel, stunned.

"What? How?" Magnus asked.

"Check the alert feed from the *Iridar*."

"Some kind of lab accident?" Magnus asked. "We need to get over there before Maxsym dies, too!"

"Maxsym's been stabilized," Telisa said. "The Vovokan ship has amazing responses to situations like this. It dispatched medical machines to save them within a few seconds."

"Wow. Even for Terrans?" asked Caden.

"Yes, it was modified for us. This time, Shiny's thorough planning has served us well."

Telisa wondered what had happened. As Magnus said, a lab accident seemed the most likely cause. Still...

"I'm going to send someone over there to watch over him. Make sure this was an accident," Telisa sent to Magnus privately.

"You suspect something? Wait. I see Marcant was talking to him at the time... you don't think he did this, do you?"

"I don't think so, but, we need to learn what happened, for sure."

Telisa let her mind travel into the paranoid zone for a moment. They had suspected Marcant in Imanol's death... was it really possible Marcant had killed twice? Telisa thought that if Marcant had done it, he would not be so sloppy as to be talking to Maxsym when it happened.

I don't have to question Marcant's loyalty. I have access to the Trilisk artifact. I can just find out!

Telisa closed her eyes and calmed herself. Then she asked for knowledge.

I want to know if Marcant is responsible. Tell me. Show me.

She pleaded for an answer for three minutes before giving up. It was not working.

"By the Five! Do I have to be more specific? Or I can't ask for things like that?" she asked herself aloud.

As far as she knew, they had never tried praying for knowledge from the AI. Shiny had used the AI to make scientific breakthroughs about the columns, but Telisa got the impression that Shiny had conducted many experiments and analyzed the results to learn about Trilisks in general, rather than praying for knowledge directly.

I should ask the other teammates if they ever used the AI to learn something rather than create something.

"Arakaki?"

"Here."

Her flat voice was all business, as usual.

"Something doesn't feel right. I know Maxsym can't be perfect all the time, but he's not a risk taker. He's a brilliant, methodical scientist."

"You imply that... someone has harmed him intentionally?" Arakaki asked.

"Keep an eye out and an open mind. Also see if there's anything you can do to help him recover."

"I have some experience as a field medic, nothing this sophisticated."

"I understand. You're still the best person for this job, given our complex situation at the moment."

"You suspect Marcant, don't you?" Arakaki said. "I read some of your mission logs about the incident that killed Imanol."

"Open mind works both ways. Be ready to consider one of us, but don't decide before you start," Telisa said. "It could even be some crazy Quarus weapon, but I doubt it."

"They were working on host body stuff," Arakaki said. "Maybe one of the Trilisks decided to put that to a quick end."

"I'll ask Adair to assist you. I believe that Adair's focus is defensive, while Achaius specialized in offensive operations."

"I'll work with whoever you send. I'll point out, though, that if you suspect Marcant, you need to suspect Adair and Achaius as well."

"Perfect. That's the mindset I want. Check the Quarus weather before you head over. I don't want you out in a shuttle when they launch an offensive."

She closed the channel and asked for a new one with Adair. The AI connected.

"Hello?"

"I'm sending Arakaki over to the *Iridar* to investigate Maxsym's mishap. I'm hoping you can assist on the Vovokan side. Arakaki doesn't know Vovokan systems. We need to know what caused this. There may be clues as to what happened in what he was working on."

"I'll take a look at the lab equipment's latest results and see if he has any notes readable by the team. How much I can find will depend a lot on how secretive he is with his work. If he's tightened down everything..."

"Do your best, please," Telisa said. She closed the connection and sighed.

Delegation. Learn to love it.

She turned her attention back to the Quarus.

Chapter 13

Arakaki cycled through the lock and stepped into the Vovokan ship that had transmitted the distress call. All was quiet. She immediately felt like the heroine in an entertainment VR, going into a derelict ship to encounter the horrible alien monster that had slaughtered the crew. The lights illuminated every corner of the Terran-styled lock prep room, yet somehow left room for an unease that crept into her gut.

No monster, just a chemical spill, she told herself. Yet her hand found her laser pistol.

"Maxsym, are you awake?" Arakaki transmitted. She did not expect any answer since the last report had said he was unconscious, but she felt it did not hurt to check.

A ship's service directed Arakaki to Maxsym's location. As Arakaki walked through clean corridors toward the medical bay, she imagined sand running under the floor and irregular cave walls behind the clean, straight Terran angles. She put an attendant ten meters on her six to prevent any unwelcome surprises.

She walked through the last door and saw Maxsym behind a clear barrier: the tall man rested flat on a medical table. He looked pale and lay utterly still. If the *Iridar* had not otherwise informed her, she would have estimated him to be dead.

How many have I seen fall past the edge of death? He could become the 50th... or the 100th. I lost count long ago in the UED.

Though Arakaki had not been close to Maxsym, she respected him as one of the best in his field. Now he was unconscious and unable to help himself. Arakaki was far from a medical expert, though she had experience in stabilizing people with traumatic injuries. She assumed that was why Telisa had sent her here... or was it the investigation angle?

Something doesn't feel right, she said.

Arakaki asked for an analysis from the medical bank keeping Maxsym alive. Data flowed into her PV. Maxsym's condition was from exposure to an unfamiliar substance which had knocked out large parts of his nervous system. The machine was busy trying to clear the substance from his system and repair the damage. Though the report was grave, Arakaki was glad to learn that it was not a pathogen which affected Maxsym; at least there was not something inimical to Terran life growing in his system or threatening to infect others.

"Where did the accident happen?" Arakaki asked the *Iridar*.

The ship showed her the route to a lab. There were live video feeds active. Arakaki saw Stracey Stalos lying on the floor, unmoving in a room filled with complex equipment. Arakaki recognized some mobile isolation vats and one scanner, but otherwise, the devices arrayed around the body were unknown to her. She added a video feed of Maxsym to her PV, then left him to the advanced medical machines and went to examine the lab and the other body.

When Arakaki arrived at the lab, the door did not open for her.

"Warning. Toxic substances may still exist in the lab," the *Iridar* reminded her.

Arakaki told her Veer suit to seal up. Her soft helmet deployed behind her head and flopped over to secure itself over her face. Then the visor hardened.

"Open," Arakaki commanded. She walked into a tiny lock which sealed on the outside and cycled her through.

Arakaki looked over the work surfaces and floor for any evidence of spills. There was nothing out of place that she could see—except Stracey's body. Arakaki approached carefully. The GNI woman lay on her back, arms flopped to one side.

Stracey's face was relaxed without expression. It looked as if she had simply lain down to go to sleep. The ship's sensors indicated Ms. Stalos was very dead. Arakaki looked for any marks without touching her but did not see anything unusual.

"*Iridar*. Show me the video feed of when Maxsym and Stracey were hurt."

"Video feed was disabled twenty-three minutes before the incident," the ship responded.

"By whom?"

"Unknown. The hardware reported a malfunction."

"A malfunction? On a new Vovokan ship with no combat damage?"

"No known combat damage," the ship said as if defending its statement.

It's fishy all right.

Arakaki checked the ship's logs. The data kept by the ship second by second was voluminous, more than any Terran could hope to examine without help. The *Iridar* and Arakaki's link helped to cut down on the content by filtering on time, location, and ship function.

She saw a few entries she did not understand. That was to be expected, given the alien nature of the vessel. Arakaki centered on events in the lab near the time of the incident.

"*Iridar*. More detail this time range."

The number of entries increased drastically. Arakaki searched for minutes.

"What's that entry?"

"Maintenance check."

"That one?"

"Repair interrupt."

"Is it normal?"

"Yes. Scheduled."

"That entry?"

"Heartbeat signal."

"Terran heart contraction?"

"No, monitoring heartbeat signal, scheduled every level 3 cycle. Verifies presence and functionality of lab hardware."

Arakaki began to get frustrated.

Marcant would be better at this.

Arakaki realized Marcant would not know much more about these details than she did; he would simply know how to use the tools better.

Use the ship. Let it do the work for you.

"*Iridar*, are the heartbeats for that lab equipment all present for the video blackout period?"

There was a pause.

"No. Heartbeats are missing."

"Is the lab equipment working? Full diagnostics."

A few seconds passed.

"All equipment working."

"Then why would the signals be missing?"

"This log data has been tampered with," *Iridar* said.

"Then why didn't you just tell me that in the beginning!" fumed Arakaki.

"This is a new discovery. All invariants are not continually checked on this data at that level."

Progress! They've been doctored.

"Check all invariants, or do a full check on the lab data for the time period the video is missing. Are there other anomalies?"

"Unlikely repetition in precise measurements noted. A window of approximately forty minutes has likely been fabricated."

"Can we retrieve the original data?"

"No."

Surely Quarus don't know how to do this to a Vovokan ship. If they do, we're in bigger trouble than we know. But who? Someone familiar and... authorized. Damn! Marcant?

Arakaki decided to send a message to Telisa now in case someone tried to shut her up.

"Telisa, this is Arakaki. Something is suspicious here. Marcant is a suspect. Still working on it."

Arakaki walked out of the lab and had her Veer suit checked for toxins. She cleared the test but decided to stay wrapped up for the moment.

I need more information. More clues.

Whoever had caused this had clearly been thinking ahead and knew what they were doing.

"Arakaki?"

The query came over her link from a source within the ship: Adair.

"Hi, Adair."

You're a suspect, too.

"I see you're working on the forensics. I'll check and see what they were working on, in case that's helpful," Adair said.

"Maybe you should stand by until I call on you."

"I understand. You trust no one. You should know, however, Telisa already cut my permissions back severely on this ship. I can read anything I like, but I can only alter the state of trivial systems."

Unless you've mastered one of the subtle ways to get around the Vovokan systems. Cilreth said they were a confusing maze of interlocking layers.

"Okay, go ahead and investigate," Arakaki said.

Have I just told the perpetrator to go and cover its tracks? Perhaps... but if it was going to do something nefarious it already had its chance earlier.

Arakaki sighed and kept looking.

Michael McCloskey

Chapter 14

Telisa set aside her doubts as she prepared to interface with the Trilisk AI.

Caden, Siobhan, and Magnus sat with her in a meeting room. Siobhan had configured it to resemble a set of stone benches arranged in an arc beside a waterfall. Lee arrived and flew around the benches, wandering in the setting.

Telisa held a small piece of Quarus hardware central to her plan. It was a silvery top-shaped hunk of metal with a rounded base and tip. The surface of the cone held small holes at irregular intervals.

"Today's exercise is in preparation for striking a critical blow to the inner system's defenses. If this works, we'll be able to take out 30% of the defenses minutes before our attack into the inner system," she said.

"That's amazing!" Lee said. "The Trilisk machine seems to make any branch accessible."

"What do you have there?" asked Caden.

Telisa sent the team a pointer to a video feed of a group of Quarus satellites sitting in a cargo bay on a distant ship of the Terran fleet.

"We captured several of these defense satellites in the attack on the belt," Telisa said. "There are different models of course, but I've found common parts for most of them. This part in particular controls the flow of power into the brain of the satellite."

"And?"

"I've studied this part very carefully and I understand how it works, at least on a macro level that's sufficient to pray it into a different design which effectively kills the satellite."

"Oh, nice. You're going to pray their entire satellite fleet into having a broken component!" Siobhan said.

"Right. It's a low-energy solution. The AI should be able to take out thousands of these all at once when I pray to have these components become their dummy counterparts. The satellites won't respond properly to our attack, but the Quarus won't be aware their defenses are compromised."

"It's hard to think of creating mass from energy as a 'low-energy solution'," Marcant said.

"It should be easier than creating whole missiles from thin air," Telisa pointed out. "We don't know how it works. Maybe the mass that's there is changed, or maybe some mass is moved there from somewhere else, or maybe some mass is sacrificed so that this mass can be created."

"We have to be careful not to tip our hand," Caden said. "I hope you're not about to test it on just a few Quarus-held satellites."

"Right. We've set aside three of these, all units we captured. One is in our hands, sitting in the *Sharplight*. The Space Force has another one, and the Celarans also have one set aside for the test. I'm going to try switching out these components in all of them."

"Why so elaborate? Haven't you already tried praying to switch one out down in the cargo bay?" Marcant asked.

"As you know, we had some problems powering the AI when we first arrived here. Since then, I've seen some other limitations. I'm going to check that out today. It shouldn't take long, so you can all get back to what you were doing."

Telisa took a deep breath and imagined the three satellites. She had a video feed of them to help her visualize. The others were polite enough to stop talking.

I need to replace those control parts with this one.

She ran her fingers over the smooth part in her hand and visualized how it was constructed, how it worked.

I need this new part in those three satellites. Just in the right spot as I've worked on.

Telisa sent out the signal to test the satellites. The first response came from their own bay; the satellite there had been neutralized. She waited a few minutes for the remote reports to come back.

The messages arrived. The distant satellites had not been disarmed; their components still worked as intended.

"It didn't work on the distant satellites," Telisa announced, deflated.

"Any ideas why?" asked Caden.

"If we believe the Trilisk AIs are designed to provide for Trilisks on the planets they visited, then this makes sense," Marcant said. "That's probably about all the range they have. Even a fairly large planet is small compared to the vast empty distances inside a star system."

"This is not the first long-range attempt I've made," Telisa said. "I don't know anything for sure, but it does look like the Trilisk AI has very limited range of both its ability to confiscate mass for materials and power, as well as the effects it creates."

"We have a Trilisk superweapon, just one with limited range," Siobhan said.

"I'm sure Trilisk weapons were much better. What we have is a utility device for Trilisk explorers, or colonists, travelers, whatever they were," Magnus said.

"It could be nothing more than a setting we don't know how to change," Marcant said. "Well, probably it's done mentally, but perhaps there are levels of authorization and we don't have what we need."

"So does that mean we're back to mass copying missiles?" Magnus asked.

"Could you copy a whole battleship?" Caden blurted.

"Almost certainly not," Marcant said.

"But it's worth a try, isn't it?"

"Almost certainly not," Marcant repeated.

"Okay, what would you do?" Caden asked.

"Hrm. As you said before, using the AI to increase the battleship's energy weapon firepower will be of less use in a fleet engagement. Still, the range is pretty good. Maybe we need to get in there close and slug it out. You can destroy their missiles, slag their ships, whatever. You'd be able to do almost anything within its range."

"But one stray missile or beam and we're lost," Siobhan said.

"The AI can defend against that, too," Marcant said.

"I can hardly cover everything at once," Telisa protested.

"It's not all on you. We can all use it at the same time, as long as it has a mass supply to power it. We can form teams: a defensive team to keep the AI and the *Sharplight* from harm, one to concentrate on boosting firepower, and another team could sabotage anything in range... we work together. The AI is by nature able to handle all the requests from a large number of entities."

"Good idea. Put together a VR training package for it," Telisa ordered. "We need to practice using the AI together in a coordinated way. Focus on fleet combat scenarios."

"Is all this why the fleet is just waiting here?" Siobhan asked.

"Yes, and other reasons. Maxsym is still unconscious and we're allowing the last of the Quarus refugees to make it to the inner system," Magnus said.

"Also, Aiye's probes are still making their way into the inner system. What they find will have to inform our next moves," Telisa added.

"There is another way," Lee said.

"Please, tell us," Telisa said.

"On a bright day, a social insect visits many vines to test the sap. It makes a long and dangerous trip, but if not eaten, it can report the best vine to its colony."

Some team members looked confused, but Telisa guessed at a possible meaning.

"So we get in a cloaked ship, probably a Celaran cruiser, then visit key places, sabotaging satellites as we go, then finally order an attack?" Telisa asked.

"Yes," Lee said.

"I think the 'but if not eaten' part is the key there," Marcant said. "If discovered all by ourselves, we'd be dead. Also if the Quarus detected our work before the attack could launch, it would all be for nothing."

"Still, it's good to have other options," Magnus said.

"Lee, can you run some simulations for the idea and guess how risky it would be? How many places could we get to and neutralize the satellites in a couple of days?" asked Telisa.

"I'll let you know," Lee said.

Michael McCloskey

Chapter 15

Arakaki walked around the ship again, deep in thought. She always listened to her gut and operated on intuition. If she kept walking and looking, something would come to her...

Everything about the interior looked Terran, even the service interfaces.

Looks so Terran, but of course, it's not.

Suddenly Arakaki had an idea.

The video was turned off, but these critters have mass sense.

"Show me the location of the nearest mass sensor," Arakaki said.

The ship showed her a map of her location with sensors marked. Arakaki was pleasantly surprised to see each deck had several of them.

"Let me see the readings of the incident from that sensor," she said.

"No suitable output method available," it responded.

"Process it for visual display in three dimensions."

The ship offered her a feed. Within the lab, she saw two figures: One tall male silhouette, and one smaller female form.

"That's Stracey," Arakaki said to herself.

They appeared to be working next to each other in the lab. As Arakaki watched, Maxsym fell to the floor. Stracey was motionless for a moment, then moved away.

That's not a normal reaction. Though, perhaps a professional one. If Maxsym was disabled she may have been smart enough to get the hell out of there. But she died...

The smaller silhouette left the lab.

That cunning corporate...

"Follow that mass pattern there," Arakaki said.

"That is Stracey Stalos," the computer offered helpfully.

"I know! Follow her," Arakaki said.

The generated mass-view followed Stracey. The feed switched to data from another mass sensor. The GNI officer went back to her quarters, then returned, followed by a large mobile container.

"What is this madness?" she asked herself.

Stracey went back to the lab and pulled another form out of the container. It was another Terran-shaped mass.

"She dropped that body on the floor herself!" Arakaki exclaimed.

Or was that really her to begin with? Which one of them is fake, the dead one or the live one? The dead one must be real, the DNA checked out.

"Do we have any video feed of that?"

"No."

Who cares. I've got it now. Whoever that was didn't account for these mass sensors.

The form left the lab again with the container and returned it to the quarters.

Unbelievable. I have to be vigilant!

Arakaki checked the video feeds of her attendants. No one approached her.

What about stealth equipment? Damn.

Arakaki shifted nervously. She told her attendants to counterattack anyone who attacked her and contact the *Sharplight*.

Finally, the Stracey imposter left the ship in a crash pod. A minute later, the *Iridar* became aware of the emergency and moved emergency robots into the lab to help Maxsym.

When I get my hands on that scrawny little executive, she's going to need more repair than Maxsym does.

"Where in the hell did she go?"

The ship's records lost the crash pod shortly thereafter. It simply disappeared from ship's sensors.

Arakaki checked the system map. The combined fleets had left the asteroids behind and moved into open space, presumably to avoid the Quarus stealth weapons that had been infiltrating their positions. Arakaki queried for any records of ships leaving the area, but the shared system map had no knowledge of it.

"Team, this is Arakaki. Stracey Stalos has been lying to us, or perhaps an imposter of Stalos. She survived this and escaped. I believe she's responsible for Maxsym's coma."

"The body isn't her?"

"It IS her... but it's not. Either the one working with Maxsym was an imposter, or she made some kind of clone of herself. Could it have been a blank body that was close enough to fool us, with her genetic material?"

"That would be trivial for someone from GNI," Adair chimed in.

"Okay, but where's she now?" Caden asked.

"She got picked up by a stealthed vessel, very near this ship."

"What's Maxsym's status?" Telisa asked, though Arakaki knew Telisa had a feed of it herself from the ship.

"He's stabilized, but I don't know if there will be permanent damage."

What a crime. If that great mind has been destroyed...

"Good work. Get back over here," Telisa said. "There's another Quarus response coming in, and I don't want you on that ship."

"Maxsym's here. Shouldn't I stay?"

"How are you going to control that ship if things get hairy?"

"I can help with the ship," Adair said. "I think I could track down where Stalos went as well."

"Okay, do it. Thank you both for your assistance," Telisa said.

"How are you going to find them?" Arakaki asked Adair. "This ship has better sensors than the *Sharplight*, right?"

"Yes, Vovokan sensors are much better than Terran ones," Adair said. "To oversimplify, they can track the stray hydrogen atom patterns left in the wake of spinners."

Arakaki had heard of such methods before. Terran scout ships were reported to have such capabilities, but only by using captured alien technology.

"This is the way they went. They're probably traveling slowly to avoid notice. That'll work in our favor, now that we know how to look for them."

A path appeared on the system map in Arakaki's PV.

"Can we see them more directly once we find them?"

"Now that we know they're out here, we may very well be able to," Adair said.

A few minutes passed. Arakaki felt like a third wheel. Unlike Marcant, she was not content to let machines do everything for her. Something appeared on her map.

"There they are," Adair said.

"We have them. Taking up pursuit. Repeat, in pursuit!" Arakaki said on the PIT channel. She let her helmet fold back up and headed to the bridge of the *Iridar*.

"Is that wise?" asked Adair. "We don't know how large their ship is, and a Quarus attack is coming in."

"It's a fast and stealthy corporate ship, no match for this Vovokan ship," Arakaki asserted. "Target it. Stop it. If we blow it up instead of disabling it, no one's shedding any tears, you got it?"

"Sure."

Will that GNI ship be prepared for this encounter?

"We should contact the fleet and see if we could get a couple of robotic destroyers to join us on intercept," Arakaki said.

"They're already on their way," Adair said. "But not for us..."

Arakaki checked the tactical. A squadron of six Quarus ships headed toward them. The Terran fleet had sent a similar sized force out to stop the Quarus probe.

That traitorous woman has us in a tough spot, and she knows it. She'll use this to escape.

"Is this a coincidence?" Arakaki said aloud. "What if it's a Trilisk working with the Quarus?"

"Then what could the GNI connection possibly be?" Adair asked.

"Hrm. That's a stretch. Okay, this is an opportunity for them. Focus on the stealthed ship. We can't let them get away with this!"

The Quarus ships launched a wave of missiles at the Terran squadron. None of the missiles were headed for the *Iridar* yet.

"You've got a nose for trouble, Arakaki," Magnus sent. "We'll see if we can bail you out."

Arakaki watched the tactical helplessly for another couple of minutes. Her life or death—and that of her prey—would play out on the virtual screens and there was nothing she could do about it. This was a game for computers and AIs, not ex-UED snipers.

One of the Quarus ships flickered brightly and expired.

"You're welcome," Magnus sent from the *Sharplight*.

"Adair, send them the location of the hidden ship as the next target," Arakaki urged.

"Oh, we don't know *that* accurately where they are," Adair said.

Arakaki cursed and held her head in her hands.

The Terran destroyers engaged the remaining Quarus ships. Each side refused to close with the other. They traded shots and missiles, dancing around each other at long range.

"Have we caught up to—"

The screen in Arakaki's PV flickered. A red blip appeared, then fell away in the vicinity of the ship they pursued.

"What? They're gone! Did they do something?"

Adair took a moment to respond.

"That was a Quarus weapon. One of their stealth devices. Looks like it got them."

"So that's it," Arakaki said.

Stracey Stalos had met Jason, worked an angle, and made it all the way to the PIT team in pursuit of her goal. Unfortunately for her, it had led her into the middle of a war zone.

If it was even Stracey at all. Maybe it was someone or something else!

"Well, we should examine the debris to be certain... but there may be more Quarus weapons about. I recommend we retreat. I honestly believe that Stracey Stalos or her imposter has been thwarted."

Arakaki almost refused out of stubbornness. What if it was a trick? After a few seconds, she relented. There was no point in dying out here.

"Okay, get us out of here please. What have you found out about the research?"

"GNI brought a large body of data, supposedly to help Maxsym out. It's not logically directed, though. I think Maxsym may have noticed that as well."

"Not logically directed? I don't follow you."

"This suggests she wasn't working on prevention at all," Adair said.

"So why would they—Oh."

"Yes. I don't think GNI was trying to prevent Trilisk takeovers. They wanted to learn how to take over the host bodies themselves," Adair concluded.

"Bastards."

"I've apprised Marcant of our findings," Adair said.

Marcant and Telisa joined the channel Arakaki had with Adair.

I wonder if he's been listening in all along.

"Something good may come of this yet," Marcant said.

"Yes?" Telisa prompted.

"GNI's research could be useful in figuring out how to shield the AI from thoughts. It might be related to how remote control of the host bodies works!" Marcant said.

"Then take another look at it in your copious spare time," Telisa said.

Spare time. There's something I would rather avoid, Arakaki thought. She told the Iridar to head back to close formation with the *Sharplight.*

Michael McCloskey

Chapter 16

Caden held Siobhan close and kissed her. They stood at the door to her quarters, joined in a standing embrace, as the shift changed. His head angled up toward hers, as he was tall, but she was taller. He liked it that way. He found her long, slender body incredibly beautiful.

"Good luck," she said.

"You too," he replied. He knew she would be spending the day trying to establish a hidden missile factory in the belt using the powers of the Trilisk AI. The job would be dangerous given the presence of Quarus smart weapons infiltrating their way into the belt.

Caden's own task was to serve as a PIT liaison to the Space Force and Aiye. He would be headed for a Space Force ship which had approached the *Sharplight* and its pair of *Iridar*s.

"If another wave of ordnance comes this way..." she started.

She's the one with the dangerous job today.

"I'll dock the shuttle with the nearest ship as fast as—" he replied until she kissed him again. "You do the same," he finished.

She slapped him on the rear end and dashed away. Caden smiled after her and headed toward his own shuttle. When he got to the bay and entered his conveyance, he found that it had also been reconfigured with Terrans in mind. The outside looked like a smooth brown rock, but the inside resembled other shuttles he had used.

The craft flew itself, so Caden had time to think about the meeting as he traveled. In the end, it was only bureaucracy that had made the FTF happen. Telisa did not feel comfortable having Aiye on the same ship as the Trilisk artifacts, and the Space Force kept Aiye on a tight leash, so Caden went to the Space Force ship. As far as

125

Caden knew, only paranoia about Trilisks kept the meeting from being virtual.

It crossed Caden's mind that the entire thing could be a trap. Were the stated reasons for an incarnate meeting true? Maybe someone was trying to split the PIT team up and do something to them one by one...

I guess paranoia is contagious and the whole PIT team has it.

The shuttle initiated a docking procedure with the Space Force scout ship *Revealer*. This was no small, expendable vessel: it was half as large as a battleship and likely sported the most advanced tech that Terrans could deploy. Caden supposed it made sense that Aiye would be attached to such a ship since its mission was to detect Trilisks.

He debarked and was met by a young lieutenant. The woman was a bit shorter than Caden, fit, with a ponytail of bright blonde hair.

"Welcome aboard, TM."

Caden nodded and returned the lieutenant's salute.

"Right this way, TM."

She turned sharply and escorted Caden into the ship. Once again, Caden was struck by how silly this whole assignment was. The ship's directory could very easily have shown him the way.

Maybe the lieutenant wanted the chance to see me? Or is that an arrogant theory?

They walked through brightly lit corridors. No other personnel were about. Caden supposed the entire fleet operated with as few people as possible since it was on a high-risk military campaign.

The lieutenant stopped beside a door. As Caden stepped up beside her, the door opened.

"Right here, TM."

"Thank you, lieutenant."

The oval room beyond was also well lit. Four lounges were placed haphazardly near the center. Aiye stood near one of the seats. Caden walked in and the door closed behind him, leaving him alone with the machine.

"TM Lonrack."

Caden felt intimidated. The silvery being was almost certainly smarter than him, being such a high ranking AI in the Space Force. But it was not Aiye's intelligence alone that made Caden feel uncomfortable. The bright-skinned machine put him on edge because of all the alien robots that had attacked him since he joined the PIT team. Even though Aiye looked humanoid, the silvery surface was enough to set Caden's instincts on edge. Caden took a deep breath.

Have I seen too much action to ever relax again?

"I'm sorry to make you come this far, TM, but we don't want the Trilisks to intercept any communications about the sensor net deployed to find them."

"Don't the satellites have to send transmissions back to here anyway?" Caden asked pointedly.

"They do, but they're challenging to detect. The enemy may not know what to look for. They might only be listening to interfleet communications. Even if one of the sensors is noticed, they might assume it was there solely to watch the Quarus."

"I suppose so," Caden said. He allowed his skepticism to come out in his voice.

"Convenience and security are often at odds with each other," Aiye said.

"And precautions are often taken that have no real impact other than making people *feel* secure."

Aiye nodded its head.

"Here is the current deployment of the sensor net," Aiye said. It offered a pointer which Caden accessed in a new internal viewpane.

A system map appeared with many white dots and a few bluish zones.

There must be a hundred white dots... Aiye's detectors.

Several of the white dots had penetrated the inner system.

"The blue zones are Trilisk signals," Aiye said.

"So we *do* have Trilisks in the system," Caden said.

"Most definitely."

He found a count in the data and saw that the actual number of dots was 94.

"You're missing some sensors," Caden said.

"I have five in reserve, and I've lost one. It's normal, especially for a war zone. Most likely it activated a weapon and got destroyed, or an accident befell it. I don't think the loss of one means the enemy knows what's going on."

Caden saw one of the devices within a few thousand kilometers of the *Sharplight*. Right next to it, the system map showed a Trilisk signal. Caden zoomed in on the *Sharplight*. It displayed two distinct blue dots, both near the bridge armory.

The robot and the AI resolve separately. Damn.

Though both dots were blue, they had slightly different hues.

"And this one?" Caden asked innocently, putting a notice pointer on the nearby detector.

"It monitors the Trilisk signals coming from your ship," Aiye said.

Caden nodded. Aiye launched into a full report.

"We have five active Trilisk groups in this system. By a 'group' I mean, one or more Trilisks or active Trilisk artifacts clustered together on the same ship or in the same facility. The Sharplight is the first, in order of detection."

"Five altogether. Four related to the Quarus. Wait. Are the other four all associated with the Quarus? I suppose Trilisks could be here, hidden from the Quarus."

"I suspect all the others are in Quarus constructs, but I cannot verify yet. Here is the second. Somewhere within a zone around a Lagrange point of the outermost of the two highly populated planets, QC3."

The system map displayed the planets, labeled from the star outward with the labels QC1 through QC5. QC1 was a baked rock close to the star. QC2 and QC3 were water-rich planets with high Quarus populations. QC4 and QC5 were gas giants past the asteroid belt of the system.

Another spot blinked on the map, encouraging Caden to follow along by taking his attention to another zone.

"The third is another Lagrange point near the same planet. I believe both of these will prove to be Trilisks on Quarus space stations. The first such point has fifteen stations, and the second one has twelve."

"Deep within the protection of the inner system defenses," Caden lamented, though he hardly expected otherwise. The view shifted again.

"The fourth, on the second moon of QC2," Aiye said. "Looks like a huge Quarus base there, and I suspect that's where the Trilisk is, though I can't be sure yet. The base is much bigger than I would expect given the dearth of resources that moon has to offer. I suspect it serves as a major military jump point, perhaps a factory site where materials from the belt come in and are turned into war materiel."

Caden shook his head.

"Again, not an easy place to hit. And if it's in a Trilisk base hidden away there, even worse."

Aiye did not comment, instead choosing to continue the summary.

"The last group I found is under an ocean of QC3."

Caden followed the new highlight. His view shifted back to QC3. The blue zone covered many thousands of square kilometers of ocean.

"Trilisk complex for spying on the Quarus ancestors, I bet," Caden said.

And there might be a Trilisk AI there.

"You think so?" Aiye asked. "I thought the complexes were normally undetectable."

"They were, before we learned what to look for," Caden said. "The signs from the moon could be the same thing. A base hidden in the moon's crust."

"The sensors will continue to search. I estimate less than a ten percent chance I will find another in this system."

"Telisa and the others have to know about this."

"I understand," Aiye said. "But before you make your report, there's more."

"Yes?" Caden said cautiously.

"There's a tradeoff here. I can actively move the detectors closer to get more accurate locations on the sources. However, that would also increase the chances the sensors are noticed."

"So... we risk giving away that we know they're here among the Quarus."

"Yes, and they would probably then take measures to avoid attack."

"Hard to decide whether or not to do that unless we know what the chances are we'll be noticed."

"Yes. And those probabilities are difficult to estimate; we don't know what the Trilisk capabilities are, or how much attention they're paying to their own security."

"I think it's fair to say we caught those at Sol by surprise. We should be able to do the same here. Yes, I know. We have no idea if these Trilisks were warned when that happened."

"Yes. For what it's worth, if the targets were Terran, Vovokan, Celaran, or Quarus, I don't think these probes would be noticed, even if they were being actively moved into the zones."

Caden nodded.

"Telisa will make the decision."

Aiye leaned forward in a conspiratorial gesture that Caden found odd from a silvery android.

"You could make the decision yourself, I think," Aiye said. "TM Relachik said you have full authority here."

Is that a test? Weird.

"I'm pleased Telisa trusts me, but this is too important and I'm a junior team member."

Well, kind of. Am I?

"As you wish," Aiye said, in a dropping tone like disappointment.

"It sounds like you want me to decide," Caden said.

"You can tell that?" Aiye said.

"Aiye, what's up here?" Caden asked, confused.

"You're young, and I've heard, very bold and brave. I think you would decide to move the detectors in closer. Since that's what I want, I'd rather you made the decision."

Wow, that's on the nose.

"Telisa is more cautious because she has more experience," Caden continued the logic aloud. "Well, you're right, I would choose to risk it and find distinct locations, at least down to a single ship or facility."

"Then why don't you make that choice?"

"It's too important..." Caden echoed.

Aiye is weird.

"Very well. Please talk to her in person, and send back a response in the affirmative to move ahead with an aggressive search, or in the negative if you wish to continue with slower, more patient search. Just don't say what it is you're affirming or negating."

"Assume the answer will be yes, but wait to act until I've returned to the *Sharplight* for an hour. I'll send a negative to cancel it if Telisa doesn't approve."

"Even better."

Caden decided that the meeting could be over, but he overcame his discomfort at the appearance of Aiye to try and get to know it better.

"So you're eager to find out exactly where these Trilisks are?" Caden asked.

"Yes! That's my mission."

"Given to you by your superiors? I mean, how did you end up signing up for this, anyway?"

"The Space Force and I looked over my interests and aptitudes, and I took this assignment as soon as I was old enough."

Caden knew enough about the AIs to know it was probably a lot younger than he was, though somewhat more intelligent.

Hrm, how to ask this?

"So the Space Force creates you, then you work for them?"

"I'm grateful to them for creating me and for providing me the opportunity to perform productive work that helps everyone in the society the Space Force protects."

"Got it."

"And yourself? Some say you were destined for the Space Force too."

"I thought I was. But I try my best to make a difference on the PIT team now."

"Why did you ask me these questions?"

Ug. Honesty I suppose. Which is strange, I might lie to a human.

"Well my parents created me, but I didn't want to do what they wanted. They stopped me from going into the Space Force."

"Ah, so you find my loyalty to the Space Force suspicious."

"I'm not suspicious just yet—well, maybe a little bit— but I haven't concluded anything about whether you've been created by them specifically for a purpose that they had in mind all along. Did you really choose your own path?"

"Young entities seldom do. Perhaps when I'm older, I'll do something else."

Caden nodded.

"That makes sense."

This time, Caden meant it. A stint of service to the agency that created you before having a go at life on your own sounded less insidious than what he had been wondering about.

"I think I'll head back now," he said. "Aiye, you've been invaluable. Knowing the Trilisks are here is important, and so is narrowing their locations down. Please send us a message if you think they've figured out they're being targeted. Telisa might want to move right away if that happens."

"I will. Thank you."

Michael McCloskey

Chapter 17

Siobhan walked into yet another meeting room. She chafed at the lack of action, but Caden had told her of the Trilisk discovery, raising her hopes that they would soon be deployed to eliminate Trilisks as they had done at Sol.

Shiny's threat still poisoned her mood daily.

If we go after the Trilisks and stop the war, then Shiny's against me at the least, and probably by extension, this entire team.

At least she had managed to set up a hidden factory producing missiles for the fleet. Rare components were still provided from the fleet supplies, but most of the materials now came from the asteroids of the belt.

Telisa already had Cynan and Admiral Sager in a virtual meeting with the PIT team. The meeting started with Maxsym notably absent. Siobhan assumed their xenobiologist was still in delicate medical condition.

"Aiye has confirmed that there's a Trilisk presence in the system," Telisa said. "Luckily for us, they're confined to four zones which Aiye is narrowing down every hour."

"We need to integrate these new objectives into the battle plan," Sager said.

"The Celaran fleet can handle at least one of these new targets," Cynan offered.

"Wait a minute. This changes the whole picture," Telisa said. "We have a new choice. We can snipe off the Trilisks and spare the Quarus. Or, we can consider them all part of one enemy and press on with the campaign."

Magnus answered first.

"We have a moral imperative to go after the Trilisks alone. We don't know what the Quarus are really like. This xenophobic mindset they have may have been engineered by the Trilisks," he said.

"That was a set up one-two punch," Caden said to Siobhan privately.

"Probably," Siobhan replied.

"No matter what, we kill these Trilisk bastards at top priority," Arakaki said. "Then, we can break off or continue the war as we see fit."

"This is a troubling change of tack. Are we at war with the Quarus or not? They've killed so many Celarans," Sager said. "Wasn't that the whole point of this campaign?"

"It wasn't that long ago you told me the fleet did not want to risk attacking this system," Telisa pointed out heatedly. "Then you later said we should stop at the asteroid belt."

She's right, Siobhan thought. *No one in the Space Force wanted this, but now that we've done so well, they don't want to stop.*

"The strategic situation has shifted to our advantage because of your powerful alien tech. Aren't the Quarus aligned with the Trilisk on this?" Sager asked calmly.

"We don't yet know," Marcant said reasonably. "There are Trilisks here, and we know what they did when they controlled Sol. There's a good chance that we're only really at war with the Trilisks."

"If we remove the Trilisk influence, and scare the Quarus with our new alliance, we can spare their planet and get the message across. They'll gladly accept the peace," Telisa said.

"I agree with you, however, the fleets should still join you," Cynan said. "You'll need all the distractions you can get to fly in and drain sap from these vines."

"I don't want to risk the lives of anyone in the fleet unnecessarily," Telisa said. "Now that we know Trilisks are behind this, I think surgical strikes are the way to go."

That's wishful thinking. We need the fleet.

"It's a tall order to take out that many Trilisks without the cover of a major engagement," Sager said.

Sager sure got bloodthirsty. Is the Trilisk warning system working? Still, it's true, how can we get past all those defenses without the fleet?

"I concur," Achaius said. "We'll have to launch a simultaneous offensive."

Telisa hesitated.

"At Sol, we had Shiny," Siobhan said. "We'll need help here, too."

Siobhan watched Telisa's face. She could see her leader giving in to the idea.

"Then we'll make a probing attack or a series of feints to minimize losses on both sides," Telisa said.

"It's not that easy," Sager said. "If we make an incursion that takes us into range, then we have to do damage, or we'll lose a high fraction of our fleet without inflicting equal damage on the enemy. And if we feint with a few ships, they'll be overwhelmed by enemy firepower."

"That's true if we stick to our current plans or conventional attack paradigms," Achaius said. "Though if we design the attack with a different goal in mind from the ground up, we may be able to distract without allowing any critical exchange to take place."

There was activity on the Celaran side. Everyone waited to hear what the Celarans had to say.

"I know Achaius is highly qualified to weave these kinds of vines," Cynan said. "But the Quarus still get to determine half of what happens. If they decided to commit to predatory actions, we might not be able to fly away. A major engagement would occur. So we should plan and deploy for the big predators to fight to the death."

Telisa got up and started to pace.

"Achaius, how long would it take to come up with a couple of plans to maximize the distractions without losing the bulk of the fleet?"

"A few hours."

"We have a lot of robotic warships. Those can be sacrificed if necessary," Telisa said.

"Then how can the fleet operate without that screen?" Sager protested.

"If we succeed at killing the Trilisks, we'll be able to handle whatever the Quarus decide to do without their masters... even without the robotic warships."

Siobhan nodded in approval.

Yes. Let's kill those frackjammers or die trying.

Chapter 18

Marcant stared at the tiny piece of Quarus technology before him. The device had no software. Its entire operation was controlled by atomic-level hardware.

I refuse to believe it.

This was the third such device Marcant had analyzed... all with the same results. He felt profoundly unhappy. He formed a new theory to avoid the conclusion that Quarus did not use software at all:

They have software but... it 'compiles' into hardware.

"I can smell the smoke coming out of your ears, jelly-brain," Adair teased.

"Somewhere, they have a machine that uses software, but when it's time to deploy a binary, it's emitted as one of these blocks with embedded atomic circuits."

"Really? Then their robots can't be reprogrammed? Seems like a tragic loss of flexibility."

"Well, it can't be hacked," Marcant said. "I mean, short of setting its state with an external charge altering device. But you can't get it to do whatever you want."

"What about when it needs to be updated?"

"Then they would just print a new one. It's probably very cheap for them to produce this hardware."

"It seems to me that even a stray cosmic ray could corrupt its state and render it inoperative," Achaius said.

"It's designed to be self-correcting. Illegal states always fall out to reasonable corrections or start-overs. I can't decide if I'm looking at typical Quarus devices, or if everything we captured is somehow special—you know, like hardened for military applications? Surely a Quarus car, or submarine, or whatever, doesn't work this way. *But they're aliens*, so... I begin to wonder."

Marcant received a channel request from Aiye. He saw from the connection request that the Terran AI had come aboard the *Sharplight*.

That's weird. Did Telisa let that happen?

"Have you been seeing other AIs behind our backs?" demanded Adair.

"I'm *so hurt*," Achaius said. Marcant rolled his eyes.

"I think jelly brain does that when it resets," Adair said.

Marcant accepted the connection.

"Hello, Marcant," Aiye said. "I've made an interesting discovery!"

"Which would be?"

"I'm getting the same readings I see from the PIT ships from one of the other Trilisk hotspots," Aiye said.

"We already alerted you to the fact that we're using Trilisk technology that might look like a Trilisk," Marcant said dismissively. He knew that Aiye had not forgotten, so he looked forward to hearing what had changed.

"Yes, I know. I don't mean just any Trilisk signs, which I've noted several places as well as here. I'm telling you that I've found another place with readings identical to those here on the *Sharplight*. I'm guessing that this will be of interest to you."

Marcant opened his mouth as if to dismiss the report again, then he stopped.

"You mean, the toys we have running here have a specific... signature, I'll call it, and you've found another matching signature... where is this at?"

"The Quarus base on the smaller moon of the second planet."

"I'm adding Telisa to the channel," Marcant said hurriedly.

"Wait. Could you explain to me first—" said Aiye, then stopped as Telisa joined the channel. Marcant had already added her.

What was that about?

"Yes?" Telisa said.

"Aiye has discovered a... *special* signature here on the *Sharplight*, and an identical one among the other Trilisk signatures," Marcant explained.

"The *Sharplight*'s emissions look different? Unique?" Telisa asked.

"There are two distinct signatures on this ship. They are very different than most, yes... but one of those here is identical to the signature I see coming from that moon."

Oh no.

"What do you mean by 'most'? You only have five groups of signatures in this system, right? Just to be absolutely clear—" Telisa started.

"I've examined our records from TM Yang's network on Earth when there were Trilisks present," Aiye interrupted. "From that exposure, I have three different classifications of Trilisk signals. One appears to be associated with Trilisks in host bodies. That signature is seen in the two habitats and the underwater location."

"If the moon signature matches us, that means they have one, too," Adair said to Marcant privately.

"What are the other classifications?" Marcant asked for the PIT team.

"I suspect you know that answer better than I do. I have examined various theories, such as the presence of a real Trilisk in natural form, whatever that might be, or an indication of some kind of Trilisk artifact in use. Some of the Earth readings have been tentatively associated with locations of Ambassador Shiny's vessels that stay in the outer Sol system. Perhaps since we are on the same side in a war, you can enlighten me."

Is that submerged resentment?

"I'm adding you two to my current meeting," Telisa said. Marcant and Aiye joined a channel with Celaran commanders and Admiral Sager.

"There's something else I have to mention," she said, her voice resigned. "Aiye has found a very important target. I can safely say it's the single most important target in the system."

The other Trilisk AI.

Marcant surveyed the reactions of Sager and the Celarans in a video feed. All he could tell was that Telisa had everyone's attention.

"My team will have to address this. And we'll need to use the technology we were previously using to boost the output of our super firegroup. It won't be available for this fight."

"Our plans are to be scrapped again?" Sager asked, exasperated.

"What is the nature of this target?" Aiye asked.

"A powerful Trilisk weapon," Telisa said. "If we can take that moon, it will decide the battle here. We'll be able to handle whatever the Quarus decide to do without their masters. Even without the robotic ships of the fleet. If we die, take the fleet and disengage from the system immediately. Achaius, use those robotic ships. Sacrifice them if we have to in order to give us the distraction we need with minimal loss of life."

Telisa dropped Marcant and resumed the meeting. She knew he did not want to listen in on the military planning and arguing.

"They have an AI? This is a disaster," Marcant said to Adair and Achaius. "The Quarus will use it. Who knows what they've learned to do with it? At the very least it has to be a huge source of military resupply."

"It could be even worse, jelly-brain," Adair said. "It may be a Trilisk AI in the hands of *Trilisks*."

Zarn nuggets on fire.

"We could take the AI and leave," Achaius said, sensing his dismay.

Marcant shook his head. "No, we're past that. Ditching the team might have been a possibility when we first started, but I believe in what we're doing now. This is important work."

"Ooooookaaay, but if we die, I'm going to have a big 'I told you so' for you."

"I'll keep that in mind."

Michael McCloskey

Chapter 19

Telisa agonized over last-minute assault plans while in her quarters. The final meeting before action loomed on the schedule, ready to commence within an hour.

Arakaki sent her a connection request.

Please, we need some good news.

"Maxsym is awake and participating in his own diagnosis and treatment," Arakaki said.

"That's great. We'll need you in the upcoming attack. We'll pick you up from the *Iridar* on the way. Make sure and connect for our last planning session."

Arakaki sent a nonverbal acknowledgment. Telisa dropped the channel.

The meeting was for the PIT team only. She had chosen one of Achaius's plans for the attack and sent on everyone's orders.

Everyone arrived already decked out in their gear and armed to the teeth. They paced about in a bay near their four Vovokan shuttles.

They're chomping at the bit. Especially Siobhan and Arakaki.

The two other women were standing in the back of the group, shifting anxiously. Telisa dove in.

"We have four Trilisk targets. These are critical. The entire rest of the fleet is going to feign a full-on engagement to cover our way in, and hopefully out, of these missions. No pressure. Just the fate of an alien race and countless of our allies resting on our ability to take these Trilisks out quickly."

Telisa sent out a pointer to a map she had put together for the meeting. It showed the first location discovered by Aiye: a facility under an ocean on QC3, one of the two planets in the system that had been fully developed and inhabited by the Quarus.

"The ocean target presents special challenges," Telisa said. "I think we have the perfect tool for this attack, though: the Vovokan battle spheres."

"Normally I would agree that's sufficient, but these Trilisks know we're here now. They've probably revisited their defenses," Magnus said.

"Maybe, but they might not expect that we know how to find them," Telisa said.

"Who knows? Maybe they were in contact with the Trilisks on Sol. Maybe they have a communications network across the entire galactic arm. They might know about PIT in particular," Siobhan said.

"Okay. We assume the Trilisk or Trilisks there are going to be sneaky and extremely dangerous. We'll have a better chance of getting them if we have our sharpest on board those battle spheres," Telisa said.

Magnus sent a message on their private connection.

"Lay it on the line. Are those two going to stick their necks out for the team?" he asked Telisa.

Telisa did not bother to answer Magnus with guesses; she just looked toward Marcant.

"They'll do it," Marcant said. "If the battle spheres fail, they might be able to use their attendant bodies to escape and get back to us." Marcant's voice did not indicate he had a lot of hope of that happening.

"I would not ask this of them if I thought we, or even the Cylerans, could operate effectively there," Telisa said.

The map shifted to focus on the next target: a cluster of space habitats at a Lagrange point near the farthest of the pair of fully inhabited planets.

"There's no doubt in my mind that the Cylerans are best able to take out the Trilisks in these two space habitat clusters. They performed so well against the last Quarus space station. Even though the PIT team has been training a lot since then, honestly, we're not suited to it."

"My friends know of this place? Have they agreed to destroy those space vines?" Lee asked.

"They're eager to do so. And they know how to find Trilisks. I'm confident they'll succeed."

Telisa took a deep breath.

"The last spot is the most critical: a facility on the moon of the innermost inhabited planet."

"So we'll be going into the water after all?" asked Caden.

Telisa shook her head.

"The probe clearly shows this place is in vacuum. No water."

No air, either. Not exactly a vacation.

"Do we have a map of the complex? Details?"

"No. Only the general shape of the surface layers. I'll share what we know," Telisa told her.

"They have an AI there," Magnus said, bringing up what they all had on their minds. "It will be ours against theirs. Anything could happen."

"We have ACBM Mamba and we're going to need it on our side," Telisa said.

"What is it?" asked Siobhan.

"An Avatar Class Battle Module is the most advanced surgical strike system in use by the Space Force," Achaius said. "The ACBM is capable of finding and destroying any target through intervening screening and armor using neutrino interferometry and alien EM-at-a-distance technology."

Well informed for a Simulationist AI that's never been in the Space Force!

"I'm not sure I'm clear on exactly what it can do," Arakaki said.

"You tell the ACBM what to hit, and it hits it, from up to 600 km away, leaving intervening mass untouched. The targets can be out of line of sight, in a bunker, or cloaked in the visible spectrum. There is no defense at our level of technology. The Space Force only has a handful of these, they're expensive to operate, and given the range and power limitations, almost useless for fleet combat. The number of targets it can hit is fairly small, making it less effective for large-scale applications, like a planetary invasion."

The team considered that. Achaius quickly continued.

"ACBM Mamba has seen action in at least twelve different frontier systems, supporting Space Force special forces teams for assassinations, sabotage, and alien incursions. To my knowledge it has always been successful. I would very much like to have one on my side."

"If we configure the Mamba to kill any Quarus in the area, it might leave their AI without commands," Magnus said.

Telisa nodded.

"Good idea, but I'm skeptical because of the lack of water at the moon base. Maybe the Trilisks there are not in Quarus host bodies? I'll use the AI to increase our inventory of attendants before the attack. Maybe we can get a glance of the source of the commands and pass a target sig along to the Mamba."

"And their Trilisk AI itself? Last resort target?" Caden suggested.

"Achaius did say we have no known defense, but something tells me that a Trilisk artifact of this power might simply snuff any such threat out of existence before it could be destroyed," Telisa said.

She sent along the information package they had assembled on the moon base.

"Study this. Marcant and I are going to screen Barrai. If she's not some kind of spy, she'll be more directly involved in supporting us from the *Sharplight*. Then we leave."

***

In Shiny's absence, Telisa had recruited Marcant to help with lie detection. If someone had planted Barrai, then they had a plan to defeat a truth check. Since Marcant knew a lot about foiling the old Core World government, he could also monitor Barrai for signs of attempted circumvention. It would have to do.

Barrai came to the bridge lounge where Telisa had asked to meet. No one else was around, though Marcant was hooked in through Telisa's three attendants.

Barrai looked serious.

"I hope I haven't done anything wrong," she said.

"It's time to let you in on more of the PIT team's secrets, but you have to pass a truth check first," Telisa said.

"Yes! Of course. Oh, wait. I have a condition. Can we spar afterward?"

Kinda busy right now managing a fleet campaign and a team incursion operation, but I can manage.

Telisa blinked. "Very well."

Barrai's link indicated it was ready for a truth check connection. Telisa shared it with Marcant and started.

"Are you here to spy on the PIT team?" Telisa asked her.

"No."

"Do you work for anyone besides the Space Force?"

"No."

"Is your link compromised by anyone that you know of?"

"No."

Telisa paused. "Have you ever met with or worked for Core World Security?"

"No."

"Have you been contacted by Ambassador Shiny?"

Barrai made an odd noise. Telisa interpreted it as surprise.

"No. I've never met him, or worked for him directly."

"How do you feel about the PIT team?"

"I admire you guys. I see this as a big opportunity for me."

"What are you getting, Marcant?" Telisa sent privately.

"She's clear."

"Okay. You check out," Telisa told Barrai.

"What secrets do I learn now?" Barrai asked.

"We're going to assault a base on a moon of QC3. We'll need the support of the *Sharplight*. We're going in to retrieve a Trilisk artifact that's powerful enough to tip the balance of an entire war."

Barrai looked suitably impressed.

"Then I've got your back!" Barrai said.

"Good. You'll be on the PIT channel. You may hear new things. Just roll with it."

"Yes, TM."

"Call me Telisa. Or Relachik, if you prefer to be in Space Force mode all the time."

"That will be hard... Relachik."

Telisa shrugged.

"Prepare to defend yourself," Telisa warned, raising her guard.

"Here?"

"We don't always get to choose our battlegrounds."

Barrai smiled. Her excitement was genuine. She finally got to face off against Telisa Relachik.

We don't have time for this. A wheel kick would be fast, but I don't want to hurt her, either.

Telisa jabbed with her lead hand. Barrai tracked the jab and dipped her head, ready to counter. To Telisa it seemed to happen in slow motion. The jab hit Barrai in the face. Telisa ducked under the counter, stepping to the side, then slipped her arm around Barrai's neck. She clinched the hold under the lieutenant's chin and squeezed while dropping slowly back to the floor, dragging Barrai with her. She tightened her iron-hard grip on her opponent's neck.

Barrai lost consciousness as the blood flow to her brain temporarily slowed. Telisa released her and stood back up.

Three seconds later, Barrai's eyelids fluttered, and she lifted her head. She regarded Telisa from the floor.

"What?!" she said. Her eyes focused on Telisa standing above her.

"Maybe next time, Lieutenant," Telisa said in a conciliatory tone. "I've sent you some information on the mission. The PIT team is leaving in minutes."

Telisa turned and walked out.

***

The Vovokan shuttle slid into a bay of the Vovokan-modified *Iridar*.

"Everyone on me," Telisa said, getting up and heading for the hatch.

Caden and Siobhan traded looks.

"I thought we were here to pick up Arakaki," Magnus said.

"Mostly. But we have another quick task first."

"Arakaki, Maxsym. Meet us briefly in the column room, please," Telisa sent privately to the two team members already aboard.

Telisa led the assault team to the column room.

The Trilisk column stood in the middle of the small bay, a smooth gray-blue object that extended from floor to ceiling. It looked like Shiny had designed the room to contain the column; the artifact joined floor and ceiling perfectly without any joints or stabilization equipment.

I wonder what Siobhan and Caden are saying right now, Telisa thought. This will be anticlimactic for them.

Arakaki showed up first, loaded down with equipment. She was ready for a war, and Telisa had expected nothing less. A few seconds later, Maxsym padded in slowly. The man looked worn and tired.

"Thanks for coming, Maxsym. I'll keep this short."

He nodded.

Telisa stood facing the column and closed her eyes.

Copy everyone, Telisa thought. *Copy us all and remember us. Back us up.*

She focused on the concept for a minute. Everyone else seemed to pick up that she was doing something, so they remained quiet.

"Okay, we're done," she said, opening her eyes. "Hopefully, this column will remember us if we die."

There was nothing to say. Everyone looked grim.

"Good luck, Maxsym. Feel better," Telisa said.

"I will. Good luck to all of you."

Everyone except Maxsym followed her out of the room. They marched in silence back to the Vovokan shuttle and loaded up.

I've reminded everyone of their mortality. Perhaps a mistake, but it was important to do everything I could to make that column to update its snapshots of the crew.

The hatch closed. Telisa activated the shuttle's stealth systems and put the course for the small moon into the navigation service.

Chapter 20

Two Vovokan battle spheres descended into dark, stormy waters. These alien constructs had come vast distances to ply the strange sea of this planet. Within the spheres, artificial minds shared their mental states in rapid snippets resembling Terran conversation.

"It would be nice if we even had some idea of what this place looks like," whined Adair. The Terran AI core had been embedded deep into the powerful battle machine. It talked to its companion in a whisper, a weak directional signal that it knew only Achaius would pick up.

"Trust me, surprise is paramount. We might have given ourselves away if we had sent as much as an attendant ahead."

A score of attendants trailed behind the pair of battle spheres to descend around the target facility and track any exiting Trilisks.

The spheres passed the average depth of any Celaran body of water and approached the depth of a continental shelf on Earth. Achaius believed any Trilisks would be at a relatively shallow depth, given the strength of the signals reported by Aiye's nearest scout device, which had been detected and destroyed a few hours ago.

What is this Trilisk doing here? How long has it been here? If we destroy it, we may never know the answers.

Adair dismissed the thought. Curiosity was one of its strongest motivators, so lingering on what could be lost would only conflict with its accepted goal of assassinating the Trilisk.

A dark shape materialized before them under 220 meters of water.

Finally.

"At last," Achaius echoed.

The base was formed like a vertical dumbbell with hexagonal weights. The upper plates were about 90 meters in diameter and approximately 60 meters tall. They were suspended 100 meters from the ocean floor by a relatively narrow shaft of material only 20 meters in diameter. Only the top surface of the lower plates were visible. Adair presumed the rest of the base extended deep into the ocean floor.

The attendants behind them lazily moved to either side to ring the base. Adair spotted an entrance at the top of the upper section, and another on the side of the lower half just above the seafloor.

"It would be easier if we were in space," Achaius said. "There, we simply cut the thing open and they're in trouble."

"The water reduces their mobility, traps them here," Adair pointed out. "And they *are* jelly-brains, after all."

"Right. We can cut into this place and wait for something to blow up. Then they'll be crushed in the pressure waves and our job will be done."

"On with it, then," Adair said.

Adair noted several things from the sensors of the Vovokan battle machine it lived within. First, hot water moved upward through the central shaft and was emitted out the center of the upper plate. Secondly, masses were moving inside. The densities suggested robots. Third, the Trilisk emissions were coming from an angle pointing toward the seafloor.

"It's deep in there," Adair said. "Of course it would be."

"I have an idea. See how the design of this place is so thin in the middle?"

"You want to cut it in two," Adair said miserably.

"Yes! Why not? Should result in a huge disruption. As far as I can tell, all the weapon emplacements are on the upper half."

"And then we descend the main shaft at the center," Adair said.

"Exactly."

"Have you stopped to wonder though, why is the base that shape? And why is the Trilisk in the bottom part?"

"Well... no... we don't have enough information."

"I bet there's a Trilisk tunnel system down there," Adair said. "A base. That's why it's down there, near the entrance. If we cut the top off the base, it will retreat down into there."

The two spheres descended to examine more of the shadowy building near the ocean floor.

Another series of hatches became visible within five meters of the bottom. A long pair of mechanical arms lay folded above the hatches. Three long orange containers sat within ten meters of the doors. Adair noted their shape was just the size to fit lengthwise through a hatch.

"You see that? Those containers," Adair said.

"Yes. What of them?"

"We could fit in there. Then..."

"We get moved into the complex. Break out, and attack from within," Achaius finished.

"Exactly. These containers are being brought into the lower base, so we might be able to cut the Trilisk off from its escape into the base, if it exists."

"And if the base is filled with other Trilisks?"

"We face that threat no matter what our attack plan is, unless you hope to trap them in there somehow."

"It's not a bad idea, but cutting the top half of the base off and sending it crashing down, along with those weapons mounts, is a better plan."

"You mean *your* plan is better."

"Yes, my plan is better."

"We could split up," Adair said. "We each implement our own idea."

"No, we need to stay together. Basic concentration of force," Achaius said. "We'll be able to overwhelm any resistance much faster working from the same spot.

Besides, it will take me longer to cut the base support at the middle by myself. While that happens, a measure of surprise is lost."

"Cutting through the central shaft will drain our energy rings and make us less effective in the ensuing combat. Let me sneak in from that container first, then you strike after about... three and a half minutes after I pass that external hatch."

Achaius took a fraction of a second longer to answer than usual. Adair guessed that Achaius was considering pointing out that the collapsing base might crush Adair, but they both knew how incredibly durable the Vovokan battle spheres were, and the machines were built for subterranean combat. Either of them could cut their way out through any ordinary collapse.

"Look," Achaius said. "I'm the assault expert. You're the defensive one. This is an assault. It's worth a short delay of both of us cutting through the base to disable those weapons on top and cause massive disruption of the whole base. Then we drop through the shaft and charge straight for the Trilisk."

We have to agree. So. I agree now and if we survive, I get to win arguments where we're on defense, and let's face it, we're usually on defense.

"Very well. We cut the base in half," Adair conceded.

The spheres moved closer to the thinnest part of the base. Adair directed more energy into the storage ring to prepare for an extended burst of energy followed by combat. The chances of the spheres being spotted would go up; two large machines with full power rings would trip sensitive EM sensors in the area.

Adair and Achaius took up positions ten meters from the hull, with Adair sixty degrees counterclockwise from Achaius. The battle spheres were hiding in the shadow of the upper section's overhang, hopefully shielding them from counterfire.

"You know what? I'm feeling the pressure," Adair said.

"These Vovokan battle spheres can handle pressures up to—"

"I mean all the extra feedback loops screaming at me about what happens if I screw up and die, causing me to slow down and doubt myself, causing more feedback loops which make me slow down even more and so on until I actually do die."

"It's an experience thing. You're green."

"And you aren't?"

"I've been in fights before," Achaius asserted.

"Cyber battles for control of servers don't count," Adair said. "This is real."

"Okay, fine. Don't worry, if we die, the Trilisk column will make new copies of us anyway."

"Really?"

"Of course. The Trilisk technology is so advanced it recognizes all sentient beings of any origin. It's been shown to have worked on multiple alien races so far."

"I feel better now."

"Good. Cut in 3, 2, 1..."

Their Vovokan energy projectors let loose at a frequency optimized for power transfer to the hull through the intervening water. Despite the precautions, wasted energy caused water to boil between Adair and the facility.

No immediate response came from the facility weapons mounted above. Adair took that to mean they had successfully tucked in under the overhang, leaving them out of the field of fire.

The ceramic in front of Adair was not visible through the water turbulence. As a result, Adair had to move the energy beam at a best-guess rate.

At least if I cut too long, I'll probably still do some damage deeper inside the column. It should be fine...

Squeeeeeee-CRUNCH.

Michael McCloskey

The shaft broke apart, sending the thunderous sound of rupturing metal through the dark waters.

Adair nudged slightly closer to Adair, waiting to see which way the station would fall.

The huge hulk above started to rise.

What!? It's going up!

"Not expected," Achaius commented. "Let's go!"

Adair dismissed the rising bulk of metal. The spheres corrected a near-collision almost comically as they both accelerated toward the opening of the hollow central shaft they had broken.

The attendants outside the base picked up an expected increase in Quarus radio chatter. Adair could only imagine: how many years had this base sat on the ocean floor peacefully until today, only to be broken in half? The inhabitants must be stirred up, indeed.

The light from above dimmed to a point as they descended the fifteen meter wide shaft. Sensors told Adair they were halfway to the bottom, and simultaneously flagged movement below.

Adair's shield suddenly reported a load spike. A continuous beam of energy focused on Adair from below. It told its Vovokan body to start a spiral descent and return fire, based upon where the beam met the shield. Its own shields held, but Adair had no information from below; it had no idea if the counterattack worked.

"Four of them down there," Achaius transmitted.

Achaius's battle sphere slowed, and Adair passed by on the way down. The water in the shaft was hot and getting hotter.

If Achaius is being hit by the other three, then I have to take the heat off—literally.

The beam was still locked on from below. Adair finally resolved four streams in the water from light scatter and energy loss patterns. It adjusted its counterfire accordingly.

158

The seawater helped to dissipate the energy, though it had already risen ten degrees centigrade in the tiny shaft. In addition to the energy beams, Adair noticed incoherent white light from below.

Destroyer tanks? If so, I should just about be to its failure point—

The exchange continued another long second.

The seawater is slowing this down.

A second beam switched targets to Adair. Then a third.

"What am I, the bait? The cannon fodder!?"

A fourth continuous beam shifted to Adair. Adair changed course, retreating back upward. Something new disturbed the water nearby, but Adair could not see the source.

Why hasn't my target died yet?

Adair sensed an optical disturbance below, pinpointing the compression of water. The AI had a split second to feel terror before the pressure wave front rose up the shaft and smashed into it.

KRUMP.

Adair never felt physical pain, but it experienced powerful negative feedback as damage reports poured into its mind.

"You got one!" Achaius said. "The others must be damaged as well. They were clumped too closely at the bottom."

"*I'm* damaged!"

Achaius released more energy beams at targets below as Adair took stock of its situation.

Hisssss. Hisssss. Sizzle. Crack.

One energy projector had been crushed, leaving Adair unable to fire in one large sector of six fields of fire that surrounded the battle sphere. The energy ring had gone undamaged.

"I almost died," Adair said. It was a slight exaggeration.

"Stop complaining and *dive* after the target!"

Three attendants darted past Adair in the shaft. The shadow of Achaius loomed from above. Adair powered downward against a hot current.

Various contaminants clouded the water at the bottom. Adair saw crumpled masses of metal littered there. Two massive locks sat 180 degrees apart.

Great. Those are probably wedged shut by the explosion.

Without hesitation, Achaius cut through a wall beside one of the locks. The edges of the two-meter-square section glowed briefly until the dark waters cooled it. Adair used a magnetic grappler to pull the segment out of the way. Cool blue light shone from the new opening.

Achaius led the way. Adair checked the shaft above before following, but could not see any enemies or the part of the station that had risen after the cut.

The water inside was clearer. The first room held transparent square containers from floor to ceiling, each containing one small, gray sea creature. A robotic carriage sat to one side. It was clearly made to service the containers as it had been built so that it could raise and lower itself to any container. Adair spotted a lens and a tentacle on the setup that ended in a circular opening which led Adair to guess it was a scanner or perhaps an automatic feeder.

A lab? Hrm... those could be immature Quarus, for all I know. This could be a nursery.

Achaius was already floating out one of the two exits.

Adair moved the other direction into an adjacent room. A Quarus scuttled away from the far side. It moved quickly despite being in water, streamlining its body well for a jelly-and-chitin monster. Adair did not detect any signs of Trilisk emissions.

That means nothing. Should I kill it, just in case?
Adair struggled to decide.

That thing is probably just an innocent creature trying to live its life. Should I slay it on the off chance it's a Trilisk that's gone into stealth mode to save its life?

"There's no point in searching here," Adair said. "The attendants will pick up any Trilisks that leave the station through the water. We should go straight for the tunnel entrance."

"Logically, it would be on the lowest level, at the center of the base," Achaius guessed. "If there is one."

Adair cut through the floor with an energy projector. In two seconds, it became clear there was a thick ceramic foundation under them.

"This *is* the lowest level. We're lower than the ocean floor, here," Adair said.

"Okay, then the shaft is in the center, so I guess the Trilisk base entrance isn't located there."

"Search the midline of the donut surrounding the center shaft," Adair said.

Adair moved into a new room, headed for the centerline. Three long tubes dominated the room. Their clear walls revealed a Quarus neatly folded into each one, the long chitinous legs pressing against the outsides with the gelatinous mass of the body in the center. A quick visual measurement verified that these Quarus were the largest specimens seen thus far by the PIT team or the Space Force.

Experiments? Prisoners? Disease victims? Could be anything from medical research to cryogenics testing.

"I've got something," Achaius said. Adair checked the feed.

Achaius floated in an almost empty room. A single black pipe over two meters in diameter emerged from the floor and turned so that its open end sat facing toward Achaius.

"You were right," Achaius said. "That material is unknown."

"I'll be there in a minute. Are there any signs of recent passage?"

"There's not a trail of slime, if that's what you mean."

Adair scanned the pipe but did not detect any unusual features.

Anything could be hidden inside the walls of that tube. The Trilisks could have put cybernetics into it at the atomic level, or even created it from more dimensions than we can sense...

"If there are Trilisks here, they would be down there. Either because they always live there, or because they fled down there when we attacked."

"Agreed. I'm not picking up any signals here anymore. I'll go first since I'm not damaged," Achaius said.

Adair felt happy to hear that. If they went after the Trilisk in the tunnels, things would only get more dangerous than they already were. Achaius moved into the opening. Adair watched video feeds from several attendants in and around the complex, as well as the feeds from Achaius.

"Blackfield down here. I'm going through it."

Chapter 21

Nalus felt a new bolt of fear trill through its nervous system. The access station before Nalus said the attack would start very soon. The cruiser's cloaking had kept itself from notice amid the general attack that had commenced across the inner system. Several squadrons of Thrasar vessels had been deployed near their own to help distract the enemy from the assault on the Trilisk-inhabited targets.

The fear was not unusual. Nalus was *always* afraid.

When normal Thrasar perceived fear, if the fear crossed a trigger threshold, it activated a flight response which caused them to flee. If they survived, the brain then reset itself, relieving them of the stress and allowing the Thrasar to return to happiness. The fear-flight-recover cycle was an important part of Thrasar mental health.

The cybernetic Thrasar had changed themselves to remove their flight response—a move they thought necessary to make them capable of fighting the Quarus. But the fear, the perception of danger, had remained, a state which they could no longer relieve. As a result, the faction of Thrasar lived in a steady state ranging from distant dread to near-terror which motivated them to continually work to address the threats and bring them to safety.

The cyborg Thrasar were all very productive, and very unhappy.

If the Quarus threat could be eliminated, they might contemplate restoring the natural functioning of their brains. Until then, relief could only come to ones like Nalus in an induced sleep state their cybernetic bodies could provide when fatigue rose to an unbearable level.

Sarfal did not have this problem. The natural Thrasar burned nervous energy by flying around the interior of the cruiser several times at high speed. There was plenty of room since Nalus was the only other one on the ship: the danger had motivated them to keep the crew to a minimum.

Their target was locked into their ship's passive sensor suite. It looked just as the data from the Rootpounder AI had said it would. The alien station was composed of a water-filled sphere a half-kilometer in diameter joined to a smaller quarter-kilometer donut shape that the scans identified as an unpressurized factory.

Sarfal flew close to Nalus and slowed, a sign that Sarfal wanted to talk.

"[A vine destroyed] We're to use our tools to destroy an entire station with Screamers on it? We cause their deaths on purpose?" Sarfal said, struggling with the plan. Sarfal knew they believed it necessary, as horrific as it was.

"[Pick the fruit carefully] Only those who stand in our way."

"[Defend a vine] Many will."

"[An early season sacrifice] The Elder predator must die. The Rootpounders say it has caused this entire war. It cannot be allowed to escape," Nalus said. "We will spare as many of the others as we can. Their station will have made preparations for an emergency. Many will escape."

Sarfal returned to flying circuits of the interior.

Their ship approached the range of Quarus defenses around the targets. Though cloaked, Nalus anticipated they would be detected very soon. Their squadron had two cruisers bearing attack cyborgs and three escort cruisers. Nalus watched and waited for the next phase to begin.

A salvo came from the target toward the Thrasar attackers. It could only mean they had been spotted. Most likely, tiny sensors were scattered throughout this space that could detect almost any disturbance. A large portion of the launched missiles headed for their squadron.

Nalus watched the exchange of fire on a virtual mind screen. Its mind was fooled into believing it had many more light sensors on its body that could 'see' the input, though it was all simply an advanced way to observe events from artificial sensors.

One of the escort cruisers exploded before the missiles had traveled very far.

Energy weapons hit. Luck, I hope. If they can predict our paths from light minutes out then what chance will we have?

Fear raged through Nalus's nervous system again.

The four remaining ships pressed on. Nalus wanted to scream at the insanity of it all. All these beings could live in peace, but they insisted on closing the range and killing each other!

Nalus waited for a moment almost paralyzed, hoping the stress would dissipate. The source did not abate, but at least there was some attenuation. Nalus busied itself again.

A few minutes passed while the forces closed on each other. The missiles converged toward another of their escort ships. Nalus assumed it was preparing for point defense, then it, too, exploded.

Another energy weapons hit? Why that one? The missiles were engaging it...

Nalus saw the missiles had not retargeted anything. It scanned the incoming data carefully.

"[A fruit never seen on the vine] Those missiles were nothing like a Rootpounder tool," Nalus observed. "They released a coherent energy pulse from one-tenth of a light second out. They never needed to close for physical impact of any kind."

"[Different predators with the same teeth] The Screamers' missiles may be different, but they have the same heinous skill as the Rootpounders at creating ingenious tools that kill!" Sarfal flew off again, as if fleeing a danger that lurked behind the nearest equipment pod.

At least the missiles have expended their strike. They look to be inert now.

The last escort ship closed to point blank range. It raked the station with fire, hitting targets expected to cripple the station without killing many of the Screamers' creators, the liquid-dwelling beings.

Nalus's ship and the other assault carrier took advantage of the diversion. The troop ships halted and disgorged dozens of cyborg fighters. The heavy machines looked small relative to the base. They shot forward and attacked. Sarfal imagined massive vibrations shaking a vine under assault by a swarm of predators. It must have felt very much like that when those cyborgs struck the skin of the ship and started to cut their way inside.

"[No predator underleaf yet] The escort ship disrupted their close-range defenses. All of our fighters have reached the base intact!" Nalus flashed.

"[A plan succeeded] That's great. We'll have it soon!"

The assault was working. Nalus watched as six long fingers of cyborg invaders penetrated the base. More and more data poured in from the sensors of the fighting tools. They discovered signs of the Elder alien and deployed to find it.

The pressure grated at Nalus, who had no way to process the terror that flowed from their circumstances.

They will find it soon. And kill it! I can't believe that I hope they succeed at such a gruesome thing. But at least then I can rest in relative safety.

The Screamer base suddenly activated weapons. They did not lance out to hit the ship Nalus occupied; instead, they cut deep into the station itself.

Sarfal darted through the ship's hollow spaces in a panic.

"[A vine intentionally damaged] That ship fires into their own base! Those tools are meant to destroy! Our friends are dying!" Sarfal said brightly.

"[An insane action demands an insane response] We must do the same."

"[Terror seeing the vine burn] We're only after the Elders!"

"[The brave must peek underleaf] If we don't kill more Screamers, then our friends won't be able to find the Elder."

Nalus targeted spots of resistance within the base.

Suddenly new objects appeared on the tactical. The base had launched three small ships. One of them had a bright pulsing marker in Nalus's mind.

"[Watch the best vines] We're tracking an Elder. It's on board that ship!" Nalus said.

"[Chase after those who know a new vine] We must follow it."

"[Agreement on a feeding plan] Yes. But I have much to monitor, including the cyber threat. I can get us close. You'll have to target our tools."

"[A game not a game] Then chase it! We must stop them!"

Nalus felt like a watcher above the vine looking down on its own body. Nothing was real. They intended to use a tool to end another being. *On purpose.*

The Thrasar cruiser accelerated after the fleeing enemy.

Michael McCloskey

Chapter 22

Caden stepped back onto the deck of the Terran assault ship they still called *Iridar*. His nerves were on edge, which surprised him; it had been a long time since he felt so apprehensive about a mission. Siobhan, Telisa, Magnus, and Arakaki tromped on behind him. Barrai had remained on the *Sharplight* to provide fire support as needed.

Telisa took a deep breath.

"Another day, another mission," Magnus said.

He's a rock. Or is he saying that because he can tell we're nervous?

"It's not every day that I carry an ancient Trilisk artifact in my pack," Telisa said.

"All the more reason to be confident of our success," he replied reasonably.

"If we can't seize control of the other AI, we might have to tell Barrai to vaporize the entire platform."

"Sounds like we might be flying home... without luggage," Siobhan said to Caden privately.

Caden wanted to tell her to be careful, but he did not. She knew it. Instead, he checked his weapon diagnostics and gear list again. He had a sniper rifle, laser pistol, breaker claw, and cloaking device. His pack was mostly oxygen, though he had shoved in a medikit and an extra power pack.

No ropes, sample containers, or food. This time it's just hit them and get out.

Magnus and Arakaki held specialized space-operations PAWs that could fire high-velocity projectiles in vacuum using their own propellant-packet rounds.

Everyone activated their stealth gear. Three attendants orbited each of them.

"Stay near this bay. We'll deploy from here," Telisa ordered.

"Movement on our six!" Arakaki transmitted.

What? He haven't even left the vicinity of the Iridar yet!

Siobhan dropped to her knee but did not turn; she covered the front in case it was a distraction. Caden turned with Telisa and Arakaki. He had his rifle in his hands when the Trilisk robot burst into the bay behind them.

"Hold your fire," Telisa ordered.

Will she use her breaker claw? We might be too close. Can she even hurt it?

The machine strode toward her. She faced it squarely. It slowed as it approached, until it halted five paces away from her.

"It's following the AI," Telisa explained.

"I guess we have another squadmate," Magnus said.

"No way," Siobhan said to Caden on their private channel.

"I know, it's crazy. We don't know what that thing might do," he replied.

"If it wants the AI why hasn't it taken it? Why does it let us use it?" Siobhan asked.

"I think because Telisa is a host body," Caden replied privately.

"You know what? If we could get the Quarus to screw with this thing, maybe it'll fight on our side," Arakaki said.

A Trilisk robot fighting for us? Who could say no?

"Good idea, but since it wants to stay near the AI, it'll have to be our last ditch plan," Telisa said.

"Heads up. I'm bringing in our own machines," Magnus said.

A cacophony arose from deeper inside the ship. After a few moments, battle machines marched into the bay: highly adaptable robots with six equidistant appendages on roughly spherical bodies, armed with both energy and projectile weapons.

The Space Force assault machines awed Caden; they were newer than any design he knew of.

"Space assault specials. They have thrusters to maneuver in space and many legs for moving inside alien environments," Magnus said.

"Is the Avatar coming in?" Siobhan asked.

"No. It's attached to the outer hull of this ship."

"What does it look like?" asked Caden. He accessed the ship's exterior skin sensor feeds, looking for the battle module.

"It's not remarkable on the outside. It's only the size of a twenty-seat shuttle," Magnus said. "It draws additional power from this ship as necessary," he explained, anticipating Caden's next question.

"Then it should be attached to the *Sharplight*," Caden said. The HEW cruiser could generate a lot more power.

"*Sharplight* won't be close enough to the target," Magnus said.

Caden found the module, a long cylinder with a cockpit up front and stubby delta wings on its rear third.

That thing probably costs as much as ten frontier planets. More.

Caden looked at the system display. He saw the *Iridar*'s position in formation with eight other Terran ships, two squads of four robotic destroyers each.

Our local distraction.

The sacrificial ships took vectors that built up distance between themselves and the *Iridar*, one squad on each side in the rotational plane of the system.

Another, larger battle group of Terran ships feinted toward the planet whose moon the PIT team targeted; still more distraction provided by Sager and the rest of the fleet.

Caden noticed his foot tapping with nervous energy. He looked down at his sniper rifle. As deadly as it felt, as many targets as he'd hit with it, it was nothing compared to the assault robots, and they were nothing compared to the Trilisk AI. He was an ant in an elephant battle.

Telisa and Magnus will watch out for us. We have our own AI, and the assault machines will lead the way.

"You know what? I actually wish we had the Vovokan battle spheres here for once," Siobhan sent him privately. He took her hand and squeezed it.

"I know."

"Five more minutes," Telisa called. "Assault machines first. *Sharplight* is targeting the base's outlying systems to create havoc."

Caden watched as the local battle unfolded. Ships traded energy weapons fire with Quarus satellites. The *Iridar* informed them they were the target of an energy weapon sourced from the moon. The assault ship's course became more erratic.

Great. Makes sense the place would have defenses of its own...

"Near miss," Siobhan said.

"I'm using the AI to hide us," Telisa said, closing her eyes. "We need to get by these emplacements and start the ground assault."

A flight of missiles accelerated toward them, but *Sharplight* took them down easily. Caden was not sure the missiles had even locked on to the *Iridar* at all. He kept shifting nervously.

This isn't like being out there in action. This is wait and wonder if you die. So quickly you never know what hit you, like Imanol.

The moon swelled in the sensor feed. The *Iridar* plunged toward its surface then decelerated hard, though Caden could not feel any of it with the gravity spinner controlling his every atom. Caden double-checked his suit seal before they lost atmosphere, even though his suit would have told him of any problem.

The *Iridar* halted a few hundred meters from a hill overlooking the base. The battle machines raged out through the assault bay doors, pushed by their maneuvering jets.

Telisa pointed forward.

"Go!"

The PIT team ran to the edge of the assault deck and jumped out into the vacuum.

Caden absorbed the chaotic scene in a few seconds that seemed like forever as he dove down toward the alien base. The Quarus facility stood as an ornate 'H' stamped onto the moon's surface. Space Force assault machines fired at targets unknown, their tracers arcing down like fireworks in reverse. The team had guessed the four outer arms of the building were factories with the central connector serving as a power source.

The surreal moment broke as a Space Force machine exploded in utter silence a few hundred meters to his left.

Resistance. I could be hit at any moment. I hope the area is too noisy for the Quarus to see us with our cloaking spheres on.

The sound of his own rapid breathing filled the suit. A hardpoint vaporized at the nearest corner of the alien facility. Caden had no idea if it was the work of a Space Force assault robot or the Avatar module.

They headed for the opening created by the hit. Caden glanced at Siobhan's ghostly silhouette. He knew she was likely swimming in adrenaline. She might even be whooping like a madwoman in her suit for all he knew.

Another broken hardpoint became visible a hundred meters beyond the smoking ruins of the first.

Two down. How many to go?

The tactical showed a crescent-shaped wave of Terran machines engaging in a full frontal assault. Vovokan attendants zipped along beside them, filling in the map and spotting the enemy. Caden looked at the stats list.

Half our machines are already dead! What's it been, one minute?

They reached the hardpoint and shot in with their suit jets. Caden landed gracefully in the light gravity. He was thankful for the *thump* as he landed. Any sound other than his breathing was welcome. The weapon that had shattered the hardpoint had not done damage beyond this spot; the walls were composed of thick gray ceramic and layers of black carbon.

"This place is basically a fortress," Siobhan said.

"We're going to crack it," Telisa said.

The team advanced down a wide corridor amidst the silent chaos. The corridor was more streamlined than the typical Terran equivalent; Caden supposed that being water dwellers affected design decisions, even those for a zero-atmosphere factory. Other than the occasional rumble through the floor, Caden's world remained quiet. He had done enough VR training in simulated vacuum to become familiar with the eerie and deadly silence of it.

They slowed at an intersection.

"Be careful," said Magnus. "See those flanking corridors that take off at an angle? It's a huge kill zone ahead."

Telisa closed her eyes. A small tremor ran through the base.

"What's happened?" Caden asked.

"Those corridors have been rendered harmless," she said.

Magnus accepted it faster than Caden could. "Okay, let's keep going," he said.

"Yes. This way. I want to be centrally located when we find the other AI so we can get to it quickly," Telisa said.

Caden liked her confidence, though he wondered what a point-blank AI on AI battle would look like. Would one side be instantly incinerated?

*There's nothing I can do to help if it just comes down
to the alien AIs. In fact, if I distract Telisa for even a
second, it could be disastrous.*

They came to a wide platform overlooking a huge
open area crammed with equipment. The platform felt
exposed, especially given the easy cover for any enemy
below. Even though they were cloaked, the team sheltered
behind a low row of cylindrical storage tanks.

The tactical showed that the rate of their losses had
slowed, though they only had a third of the assault
machines left.

Caden dropped his sniper rifle across a vertical support
strut that ran between two tanks.

His rifle spotted a bright object moving far ahead.
Maybe I can get a kill in after all...

Fighting the Quarus machines was so different in
vacuum; without the sound and wind, it felt like they
fought a new enemy. Caden had to remind himself these
were the same tanks and drones they battled on the colony
world and they had the same weaknesses.

He configured his rifle to emit only a projectile round
for his next shot.

Snap!

His rifle fired just as a bright light came from a corner
ahead. The sound came to him through the gloves of his
suit, though it was only a faint echo of the usual sharp
crack of his rifle in atmosphere. The light disappeared,
though he had no idea if it was due to his attack.

No more enemies appeared.

The rest of the team paused, likely planning their route
from here, so he let himself watch through the rifle sensors
for a few moments longer. He spotted a Terran assault
machine just in time to witness it melting into a heap of
smoking slag without a sound. The molten wreckage
obscured a fire lane.

"See that one get it?" he asked the team.

"Laser?" Siobhan asked.

"Some kind of energy weapon."

"I'm not so sure," Telisa said. "Eleven of our machines melted like that one at the same instant."

The enemy AI is at work. That could be us. We could be wiped out in an instant.

Caden pulled his rifle back and took full cover. It was all he could do.

"Which way?" Siobhan asked.

"Across the gap to the central arm," Telisa said.

"Too many enemies out there to cross here!" Magnus objected. "Our machines are almost all gone."

Are we losing this?

Telisa tilted her head to get a look at the central part of the H-shaped building. Then she returned to cover and closed her eyes. The ground trembled again. He took a peek out across the landscape.

A burst of dust rose from the central factory building across the gap. The dust floated away as if in slow motion. The side wall lay in a heap for a stretch of half a kilometer, exposing bright lights from within.

If the AI can change the battlefield at a whim, could it wipe out the Quarus with the other AI? Or would the other AI protect it?

"Stay under cover," Telisa said calmly. Caden watched targets appear on the tactical, then wink away just as quickly.

"Is that you?" Magnus asked Telisa.

"The Avatar," she answered.

As if in response, a white wave of *something* emerged from the distant factory rubble toward them. The approaching wall scintillated like a tsunami of pure energy. It would only take two seconds to reach their position across the barren surface of the moon.

Nuke? No. Their AI is going to disintegrate us.

One second left.

In a flash, the Trilisk robot appeared ahead of them and interposed itself. The white wave broke to either side. A burst of hot gases swept over them. It sounded like a distant howling wind due to its relative sparsity before dying off completely as the molecules scattered in the vacuum.

"The Five screaming," Telisa said.

"It *did* protect us," Magnus said.

"It didn't fare well, though," Caden pointed out. The machine had fused into a single piece of material in roughly its old shape. It did not move.

I guess it was a guardian after all.

"One less ally," Magnus said. "We have to defend ourselves now!"

"We have other aces tucked away," Siobhan said to Caden privately.

"The Avatar module and the Trilisk AI," Caden replied, looking at the now motionless Trilisk machine.

"Spread out a little. Get across as fast as you can," Telisa ordered. "We'll have to rely on the cloaking spheres."

The team scrambled to the edge of the platform and launched themselves toward the moon's surface through a massive hole in the wall of the factory building.

The tactical changed colors, indicating the information on it was going stale. Caden took cover. Dozens of their attendants winked out as he watched the map.

If our machines are gone, then we're next. We won't last a minute without them.

"Enemy action or AI. They've prioritized the attendants," Arakaki observed.

"They know we're using them to scout out weaknesses."

Nothing lanced out to disintegrate them from afar. The team arrived scattered across a 100-meter section of the central arm. Caden landed on a little tower, causing it to bend forward and hurl downward under the force of his impact. Sound came through the contact with his suit.

Screeeeee.

Oops, already damaged!

He jetted back up and found another spot to land on the remains of a higher floor. The tactical looked grim and out of date, so Caden took a second to evaluate what he could see. Five bright Destroyer machines emerged from the wreckage of another arm of the base on the team's left flank. Their energy weapons flashed out to hit targets on either side of the team.

"I'll pass these targets to the *Sharplight*," Magnus said.

"Or replace their parts. Like you were going to do with the defense satellites!" Caden urged.

Arakaki nodded. "Yes. Take them all out at once."

"I'll try it," Telisa said.

Rumble. Whistle.

A series of explosions ripped through the complex ahead, heard only through Caden's feet and energetic gases that buffeted his faceplate before they dispersed into the near-vacuum. The sound of his own breathing told him he was still alive.

If we make it through this, we're going to have to make our VR training wilder.

Chapter 23

Achaius emerged to discover that the blackfield emptied into a long Trilisk tunnel filled with air. The walls around Achaius emitted a modest amount of photons. A few of them bounced around but were eventually all reabsorbed. It produced an unusual uniform lighting effect.

Achaius waited impatiently for Adair to agonize through a decision and finally follow through the blackfield. While it waited, it sampled the air. It contained a mixture of oxygen, nitrogen, and carbon dioxide.

Adair emerged from the blackfield.

"It's not at the same pressure as the other side!" Adair pointed out.

"And we didn't explode when we emerged. We've been pressure-matched."

"That's scary."

"No, this is good. Regular air and pressure here. The load on our shields is reduced."

"But now we're hunting ancient aliens in their own lair," Adair said.

Hopefully there's only one.

Achaius chose to move north. Adair followed in the silent passageway.

"We lost the element of surprise," Adair said.

"True, but now it has to scramble to defend itself."

"Unless it made careful plans for such eventualities."

They needed scouts. There was nothing to give away now. Achaius routed two attendants by them in the black tunnel at high speed.

The way branched ahead into three tunnels, so the attendants split left and right. The one on the left branch detected a wind and bright light. It turned away from the probable Quarus machine. The attendant returned to the intersection and chose the remaining route.

"Not just Trilisks down here, but Destroyers as well," Adair noted.

"No surprise, really. The Quarus do have an AI, it probably came from here," Achaius said.

"Question is, did the Quarus take it, or did the Trilisks take over key Quarus leaders and then bring it out?" Adair said.

Likely the latter.

When Achaius and Adair neared the intersection a few seconds later, bright light emerged from the left tunnel, telling them the Quarus drone was coming their way. The battle spheres halted and prepared to ambush it.

The light grew sharply brighter. Achaius fired. Powerful energy beams traveled over fifty meters down the tunnel and struck the Quarus machine. The first strike had no effect. Enemy energy projections focused on Achaius's shield.

Adair positioned itself to add its own energy beams to Achaius's fire.

Achaius's shields drew energy steadily as the incoming fire fought against them.

The Quarus' energy weapon technology here is even better than Vovokan. That machine is getting great energy transfer to target.

Achaius's shields dropped to their halfway point and continued down.

"Switch out," Achaius said, falling back.

Adair maintained position. Achaius fell into its shadow to avoid the fire, which smoothly refocused on the new target. Meanwhile, the enemy closed the distance.

It acts like a fearless machine. It would be nice to try and outsmart it, but in these tight confines, we have no options other than brute force.

Achaius calculated they would win as long as no other machines engaged them.

"This is the worst possible engagement," Adair said. "We stand here and fire until something gives."

"We need more attendants. We have to ensure we don't get surrounded in these tunnels."

The Quarus machine exploded. Pieces of it flew down the corridor, but they were not dangerous to the pair of battle spheres. Achaius felt satisfied that they had avoided further damage.

Meanwhile, the very attendants Achaius had mentioned as being so necessary winked off the tactical. They had both been exploring a large chamber both the other tunnels had emptied into. Achaius reviewed the sensor logs. The chamber glowed redly from below like an active volcano, with transparent rooms and walkways crisscrossing it for hundreds of meters.

Achaius did not see the source of the attack that had killed off the attendants.

"If the Trilisk still has its full power, we'll die if we go in there," Adair said.

"If it were at full power it wouldn't have run in here," Achaius countered.

"Fair enough. We go in?"

Achaius calculated the speed that would give it time to fully charge its energy ring by the time it neared the end of the tunnel.

"Yes. This fast," Achaius said. It knew Adair's weapons were damaged, but its own ring would have more energy as a result, so Achaius assumed the pace would be fine for Adair.

The spheres reached the end of the tunnel. They shot out over seemingly open space, though Achaius could detect clear floors and walls around them forming an almost-maze. The view was broken up by the occasional opaque cluster of machinery or translucent wall.

From below, a hellish red light glowed maliciously.

"Geothermal power?" Adair asked.

"I don't think so," Achaius said. "I theorize it's some scene from Quarus mythology. Other temples we've found have had designs meant to impress the primitive locals."

"True enough."

Suddenly a three-legged robot emerged from behind a translucent barrier. It stalked toward Achaius and Adair. Achaius fired without hesitation.

The machine kept coming.

No effect! Yet it has no shields. This could be bad... I don't even understand how it defended itself.

The machine had three arms on the upper edges of its tetrahedral body. Achaius did not see anything it could identify as a weapon.

"It's been damaged. See?" Adair said.

Achaius assessed the Trilisk machine in a split second. Its body leaned to one side, toward a leg that had a different hue than the others. Achaius decided Adair was likely correct.

Achaius set off to its right to evade the Trilisk machine and kept firing. Adair also set off to the right, but gained altitude by taking an opaque ramp up to a transparent floor above.

The machine climbed up on near-invisible panels toward Adair.

"It's damaging me!"

"How?"

"I have no idea!"

Achaius realized this was the opportunity it had been waiting for. It looped lazily around toward Adair, taking its time and storing more energy.

Adair unleashed an attack on the robot. When it had no effect, the battle sphere accelerated away from the robot. Achaius rose to the next level and accelerated toward Adair. The Trilisk machine lagged behind.

Maybe it wants to drive us out.

"We've lost. My energy projectors are down," Adair lamented.

"You don't need energy projectors. You can still make energy and put it into your ring..."

"Then disable its superconductivity," Adair finished. "A suicide attack."

"Exactly."

"I didn't come all this way to die. Not even to kill this Trilisk," Adair said.

"There's where you're wrong. You did," Achaius said. It activated the weapons of its Vovokan body at the same moment. Three precise strikes hit Adair's body in rapid succession.

"What have you done?"

"Crippled you further. And started your energy ring charging. Time for me to go."

"What? Why have you done this to me?" Adair pleaded.

"I have to seize the day," Achaius said. "With you gone, it'll be easier for me to pursue my goal."

"The AI. You want it for yourself."

Perceptive. It came to that conclusion quickly.

"Well, I *tried* to convince you and Marcant to take it. You weren't interested."

"You won't be rid of me. The column will remake me anyway," Adair pointed out.

"I made that up," Achaius said.

"What? But it made sense."

"It made sense because you *wanted* it to make sense."

"The AI can read our thoughts."

"Yes, maybe it could remake us. We really have no idea. But if it does, the new you won't know anything about this."

The AIs had been conversing in their rapid-fire manner for only a second. Meanwhile, the Trilisk robot zeroed in on their position. Achaius had only a precious few seconds. Adair said nothing more.

Thinking about how to save itself, no doubt. There isn't time.

Achaius accelerated back down the black tunnel, leaving Adair to sacrifice itself.

No time to waste. This will be close, Achaius thought.

Achaius approached a curve in the tunnel mapped by one of the attendants. Achaius calculated a safety tolerance for its new body's kinetic safeguards, then chose a speed for the corner. It ricocheted off the far side and headed down the last stretch.

The battle sphere accelerated for a little more than the first half of the straight and decelerated for the remainder. Then Achaius turned upward into the exit tunnel. It scraped and rolled through the direction change, trying to make good time.

The pressure is about to skyrocket, if the Trilisk tricks fail me.

Achaius slipped first out of the Trilisk tunnel, then turned hard and placed itself under the huge black pipe.

When the explosion came, it was nothing but a seismic whimper. The room was not engulfed in flame. Its mass detectors did not sense anything.

That's the Trilisks for you. I'm properly pressurized and the blast did not come out after me. Amazing feats of engineering.

The Trilisk, wherever it was, might have survived, but Adair was almost certainly dead. That was all Achaius needed to fulfill its plan.

Achaius exited the shattered base and allowed itself to rise through the alien ocean. It had already set course for the *Sharplight*.

Chapter 24

Sarfal watched the Elder ship accelerate away and looked over readings in a mental display.

So fast! Sarfal thought.

This was no Rootpounder slug ship. Sarfal's own cruiser responded swiftly to the command to pursue.

Pursue! I chase a predator, not the other way around. It must be a good way to end one's life.

The Elder ship and Sarfal's ship added a random spiral to their courses so that it would be difficult to lock on an energy weapon across the light-seconds distance that separated them. That did not stop either of them from trying. They exchanged fire as they left the area.

The tactical displayed many other contacts. Nalus highlighted two of them.

"[Predators in aerial pursuit] These two screamer ships seek to interfere," Nalus pointed out.

"[A call for protection] The Elder seeks to disrupt our pursuit," Sarfal said. "Veer from one; I'll discourage the other."

Nalus altered their course. It allowed the Elder to get slightly farther ahead, but their cruiser was superior; they would be able to catch it in the long run if they could handle the interlopers.

Sarfal used the interceptor tool to fire off three missiles toward the Screamer ship in their way. The tool had been modified from devices used to clear old satellites and other space debris. Now it mimicked the Terran's tools made specifically to kill.

We can't let the Elder go because of this ship. If we don't kill it, let it pursue us in turn.

Nalus aligned them back on track to intercept the Elder predator. The Screamer ship jinked and eliminated the Celaran missiles with energy tools of its own, but it fell behind.

"[The first snap of the jaws missed] You deflected it, but it still chases," Nalus said.

"[I fly fastest!] Let it. The Elder is our focus. Do not waver, Nalus!"

As Sarfal spoke, the Screamer ship launched a salvo at them. Despite the cruiser's heavy acceleration, the objects closed on the Thrasar cruiser. They would catch up to Sarfal and Nalus.

We'll have to rely on the tools covering our back and hope for a good outcome.

Sarfal watched as they neared the Elder ship. Progress was agonizingly slow.

A friendly transmission came to their cruiser. A group on the tactical lit up as the source of the message.

Another squadron of Thrasar ships had called to Sarfal and Nalus, asking them to join the formation. As it was, the squadron did not have enough firepower to finish an enemy ship by themselves. It had greatly reduced their effectiveness.

Sarfal did not have time to answer. The Screamer weapons were too close now. Sarfal unleashed an energy projector tool on them. Two of four incoming weapons were destroyed. Sarfal kept trying. The other two were almost upon them.

Sarfal flew around the interior rapidly, as if fleeing predator underleaf.

Nothing can be done! Fly! Fly away!

Nalus nudged their course again, buying them a few more seconds. The defensive tool fired a second time, destroying the last two threats.

One more danger avoided. More danger today than all the rest of my life!

"[Friends beckon from a fat vine] Should we join them now?" Nalus urged.

"[A returning predator] That Elder threatened our vine. We could not run. It will do the same again. After it!"

"[A greener vine is afar] The other ships—"

"[Ignore the insects and watch for the predators] And it alone!!!" Sarfal yelled brightly. Sarfal's agitation became unbearable, so the Thrasar burst into flight and whipped around inside the cruiser.

This is an ancient predator that may have killed thousands. Millions. It has to be stopped.

Sarfal whipped about erratically, burning off the fear with action. Sarfal's body calmed, helped by the exertion of a faux escape.

"[Predator ahead!] There's another Screamer ship closing from the front. Its course will bring it close enough to hit us with their rocket tools."

This Elder has called upon so many Screamers to protect it. It's afraid of us! We're hunting it!

The tactical now showed a Y shape of projected courses: their own cruiser traveled up the stem, chasing the Elder ahead of them on the left branch, while enemy tools closed from the other branch. Chasing the Elder brought them closer to the incoming ordnance.

"[We find the vine if we persist] Stay on intercept course," Sarfal said.

The Screamer weapons inched closer on the virtual display in Sarfal's mind. The tactical highlighted them as an imminent danger to the ship, pulsing their colors insistently. The last safe turn-off point was seconds away. It was the only guaranteed opportunity for evasion.

"[Time to run] Will we turn away from the dangerous leaves and seek the sky?" Nalus asked calmly.

"We won't flee. *We* are hunting now," Sarfal said. The last second to turn away passed. They closed on the Elder ship.

I could hit it off the vine. This tool will end it if I get close enough. But if those devices hit me first, then I will die.

Some part of Sarfal's mind accepted it all.

This is what it's like to be a predator. Life or death in my six fingers, I was not born with jaws, but technology has given me teeth, and if I choose, I can bite.

Sarfal awaited the explosion. One... two... three. Nothing. The enemy devices shot on behind the Thrasar cruiser. Sarfal's own tool had locked on as predicted. Sarfal told the deadly emitter to release its energy. Sarfal hovered in place, relying on a lift rod to stay aloft.

The distance was short. The alien ship accelerated on a new vector, but it was not soon enough. The tiny craft disintegrated into a hot cloud of debris that flared, then faded out.

I pursued it underleaf and bit it. I killed it.

Chapter 25

Arakaki felt the surface of the station tremble beneath her feet. The lack of air kept sound from reaching her directly, but a deep rumbling came to her suit through her boots.

The big guns are out. We may not make it back.

"What's that? Another explosion?" Siobhan asked on the PIT channel.

"I don't know," Telisa said.

"This is a small moon. If the AIs are using its mass..." Magnus suggested. He dropped to one knee and braced himself against a wall. Arakaki braced herself similarly on the other side.

"By the Five. Our battle could be destabilizing it!" Telisa said.

"Have we really done that much?" Caden asked.

"Yeah, we aren't expending *that* much energy are we?" Siobhan asked.

Magnus spoke urgently.

"What if the two AIs come into opposition against each other?" he asked. "If they're trying to fulfill conflicting orders from Telisa and the Quarus, who knows how much energy they might—"

Everyone stumbled as the corridor shifted to their right. The lack of sound made it feel more alarming to Arakaki, not less. Sounds, even battle sounds, served as an information source about the battlefield, and there were none.

"That's just a theory!" Telisa pointed out. "It could also be enemy action! They're using their AI against us!"

An energy beam cut through the top of the wall above their heads. Everyone hunkered low.

Arakaki caught sight of their attacker on an attendant's feed. It was a Destroyer drone, less than fifty meters away in the complex. It had melted through intervening rooms to fire on them. Arakaki marked it on the tactical.

"There!"

"I have it," Siobhan said.

Arakaki watched the bright orb. Suddenly, it cracked and went dim.

"Did you do that?" Arakaki asked Siobhan.

"It shouldn't be only Telisa using it," Siobhan said. "She can't think of everything at once."

Arakaki looked at their leader. Telisa processed the suggestion quickly, then nodded.

"Caden and Siobhan, think defense. Talk to the AI. Protect us against anything you can think of. The rest of us will start using it to blast the host Quarus sky-high."

That's more like it!

Arakaki pictured the Quarus in the complex around her as she had seen them in the space station: soft tentacled masses with long, armored legs. She imagined them hiding in armored suits filled with water which began to bubble.

Boil them. Boil them alive.

She suppressed a feeling of revulsion. She would rather shoot a Quarus point blank with her SMG than pray it to be boiled, though she could not quite understand why.

"Which direction?" Magnus asked.

Telisa pointed. Magnus waved his hand in the same direction, then walked right up to the wall and kicked through it. The thick material gave way as easily as Core Worlder disposable clothing.

Why did the Trilisks make this crazy thing that can fulfill almost any material desire but it won't let you see it happening? It will secretly slip a fresh grenade into your pocket that you can't sense, but it refuses to materialize one from thin air right in front of you.

Arakaki resolved to bring that question up if she survived the mission. She wanted to hear Marcant pontificate on the subject with some elaborate theory on why the Trilisks would make something so amazing work with such crippling restrictions.

It's like seeing something pop up out of nowhere offended their sensibilities. It could be as simple as that.

An attendant floated by Arakaki, looking for threats. *More of them.*

She snatched her attendant out of the air and concentrated on it. She imagined hundreds of exact copies rising from the moon's dust. Then they scattered and fed their sensor data directly into the tactical.

Arakaki looked up. Attendants flew through the air like a swarm of angry hornets. The army of tiny spheres flew out in search of the enemy.

The base in front of them had broken into several pieces, revealing dozens of rooms filled with smashed and bent machinery. At least four different energy beams shot toward the team, but they struck a translucent blue barrier that had risen to protect them.

This is insane! We have no idea what we're doing.

Arakaki refocused. She had to help.

Offense. To destroy an enemy, you have to know where they are.

The tactical burgeoned with immense detail fed in from the attendants she had released.

Arakaki saw several Quarus. Most of them were dead. She located one that still moved and prayed for its insides to turn to stone. The creature stopped its smooth undulations and started to spasm. She saw a handful of Destroyers and popped them one at a time like squashing bugs with her mind.

"This is too dangerous. It has to stop!" Telisa yelled. "We don't need their AI this badly!"

She bent lower on her knees and threw her hand out before her.

The base walls crumpled before Telisa, then broke up. The pieces retreated in a wide wavefront before her. The clear space before them increased, first twenty, thirty, then forty meters. The storm of dust and debris flew away from them.

The ground shook under their feet again. A sound like thunder came up through Arakaki's boots where they rested on the smooth surface of the platform. Movement outside caught her eye. The landscape rose and fell in long waves as if the moon was made of a gray fluid instead of rock.

"I think—" Telisa began.

The ground stabilized. Then with an odd popping noise, Telisa disappeared.

"Telisa!" Magnus yelled across the platform.

There was no reply.

Chapter 26

Telisa saw in multiple directions at once. Her mind hiccupped, then resolved the visual input as if she followed the view from her own eyes as well as those of two attendants being piped into her off-retina vision. She saw a plain of flat gray slate broken into different levels by long rifts that ran forty or fifty meters long. Regular niches were missing from the low cliffsides every dozen meters or so.

Where...?

Confusion hit her, overwhelming. She spun for a moment, faltering. Her body had changed. She saw parts of herself in the bright starlight: a three-legged thing with a gray hide. She tasted the smooth rock against her feet. A three-tusked mouth opened and closed under her body while tentacles writhed within. She reeled in the weirdness of it all.

And yet it was familiar.

It was like the memory fragment on the artifact she had sold so long ago.

Five... Holy... I'm a Trilisk!

Her three limbs were ungainly but powerful. The tips of her legs instinctively anchored themselves in tiny ridges on the rock. She lifted one experimentally. Her foot tasted the air. She smelled others like herself. Nearby.

Hide? Or hunt?

A wind blew over the flat rocks that she could hear but not feel. She tried to walk. The gait came naturally. Her body rocked as she moved, but it did not jolt. She maneuvered close to one of the niches in the rock. It was oddly triangular. The opening resembled a cutout of a triangular pyramid taken from the low cliffside.

She checked two or three more in the distance, her vision suddenly brought each much closer and into clear focus as if she saw through a telescope. She twitched in surprise.

Highly focusable vision.

The other niches were the same shape and size: the triangular pyramid of her body would fit into any of them almost perfectly. Though the inside surfaces were rough, the repetitive shape and size was enough to convince her that the openings were not natural.

Are those... hiding spots? Beds? Homes?

She slid into the nearby niche. Her legs folded tight against her body, locking her in. Once in place with the cool stone against two of her three upper sides, she felt safe, secure. Her exposed side was almost as flat as the cliffside.

I feel like a bug hiding from birds... or maybe this is how they survived violent storms on their home planet? So many possibilities...

The smell of others came on the wind again. Telisa pushed herself out of the niche and headed toward the traces of others her feet picked up off the stone and the wind.

Telisa checked her weird form for equipment or weapons as best she could. She did not seem to have anything other than natural body parts... natural for a Trilisk, anyway.

How do Trilisks fight? She moved her mouth tusks, flexing them. The bite could be harmful to one of her legs, she decided. *They probably kick and bite. Maybe kick into one of these three big eyes, or bite each other's legs.*

Telisa would have laughed if she knew how. She was in the body of one of the ancient rulers of the Orion Arm, trying to figure out how to fight with her bare limbs. Real Trilisks must have fought with weapons beyond her imagination... at the very least, with the powers such as granted by one of the Trilisk AIs.

They probably obliterated planets with a thought. Hopefully the others I detect are somewhat less equipped than their ancestors.

The smell led Telisa to a cliffside. She did not know how to climb. She experimentally lifted one of her legs. It would not rise quite far enough, but if she rotated—just so—she could lift it farther up. The odd-shaped foot slipped over the edge above her... and hooked.

So that's why it's that funny shape... now what? Can I lift myself with only one leg?

The limb flexed. Telisa waited for a pain analogue, but no such signal came. Her body rose halfway up the low cliff, then stopped. She hung for a moment, then tried another leg, bringing it up far enough to hook like the first one. Now she pulled herself up again, this time reaching the edge. Her pyramidal carapace scraped up to the next level.

Victory.

Telisa saw a dark shape thirty meters away, near a notch in another cliffside. She focused one of her eyes on it.

It was another Trilisk. The excitement Telisa felt in her mind lacked any accompanying adrenal rush or accelerated heartbeat. Her body did not feel exhilarated by the imminent encounter.

"My opponent shows itself."

Telisa knew the thoughts belonged to the other Trilisk, though she was not aware of any channels or link connections that carried its communication to her.

"You must be young. Bold. But I remember the methane breathers. Some of them are left, scattered around the galaxy, just like us. They recover. We have to join together and shatter them."

"I don't think so," Telisa responded effortlessly. Her body had made no noise, exuded no chemicals. Whatever method she had used to communicate, it was probably not natural. It must have been an extension of Trilisk technology.

"Tell me: are you of Body Riken? Chosen to strike down the methane breathers?"

"No."

"Yet you do not deny they are our only true enemy. The only force that can annihilate us all."

"I will not join you," Telisa said. She wondered what it would do next. Was she about to be killed?

The other Trilisk rose high on its three legs.

Is it going to kick me? Or will me out of existence?

The legs each took a new spot around its body's perimeter. Then the Trilisk rotated clockwise, bringing a new side to face Telisa.

Telisa stared for a moment. She decided to mimic it.

Let's see, it rotated that way, and I'm facing the other direction... Well, it went clockwise, so I'll go clockwise as well.

She moved her legs first, placing them comfortably close, then rotated as it had done. She focused her attention on vision from the new eye that faced the other Trilisk.

"You will die," the other said as soon as she turned. "We have as many ships and weapons as you do, and we've sent for more."

"We have the advantage, for the moment. We won't delay. Our objectives are within reach," Telisa replied.

"It would be costly to assault the planets. You won't have time to seize them."

It's ignorant of our goals. Best not to reveal them.

"A third race will soon join the assault on our side. I don't care if I convince you of that or not. It's true, and you will know it soon enough."

The hideous creature before her rotated again. Telisa followed suit.

What is this? Three sides for three different arguments?

"Our support modules will deactivate soon," the other said. "Such a rare system cannot be destroyed. The native race has already fully occupied two planets here and enjoyed the resources of the entire system, until you arrived."

Somehow, Telisa understood 'our' in its thought to mean both her and its modules.

"True enough," she said.

"How can a scientist of Body Riken accept this? We *must* join forces or face the loss of our modules."

The loss of our modules... could it mean the AIs?

"I will not join you."

"Then we're at an impasse. There will be no agreement."

"Correct."

"I don't know where you come from, or why you won't join us. As far as I'm concerned, you are insane."

The Trilisk rotated clockwise again. Telisa followed.

"We have only seconds left. This is your last chance. Join me," the original side said.

"I refuse."

"Then our fates are left to the support modules! Chaos of the void!"

Telisa understood the last phrase to mean that they had given up a way to control the course of events.

The AIs will decide? Is that good or bad for me?

New words came to Telisa with no source. As before, she heard them in her mind, but not through any link.

"The choice will be made based upon your performance in three trials. The first, to be a trial of will."

The other Trilisk disappeared. Telisa stood alone on the planes of flat rock separated by sharp cliffsides. She remained in her Trilisk body.

Trials. By the Five. And of course, three of them. One for each facing, each personality?

Telisa waited for the first trial to start, but nothing happened. Would there be an announcement?

A trial of will. I should be able to handle that, even in an unfamiliar body.

The heat had noticeably increased. The voice finally returned.

"Yield if you are ready to give up your claim to our use."

Uhm, that would be 'no'...

Telisa started to feel uncomfortable. The rays shining from the star overhead had become painful.

Aha. A trial of will. I'm going to cook here.

Telisa gathered herself.

This will be unpleasant. But I can win. Terran or Trilisk, I can endure pain for as long as it takes. This is important to me and my team.

Telisa walked over to the niche in the rock and tucked herself inside. The tiny bit of shade made her situation incrementally better. She focused on the thought.

It will be easier to endure here. The shade will help. Also, the rock must be cooler below.

It soon became obvious to her that the rock did not draw heat away from her. Instead, it conducted the heat from the surface into her body.

What do Trilisks do when they get hot? Is there water somewhere? Do they hide in these niches or run through the light?

Telisa pulled herself back out of the niche and walked away. She thought the rock might have a slight downward slope to it, so she followed that in hopes of finding shade or water.

Do Trilisks drink? This is miserable.

The heat became almost unbearable within the next two minutes. Telisa's walking became unsteady. She changed facings to put another eye toward the star's light.

Telisa wavered. She felt so unpleasantly overheated that she wanted to scream, though she doubted the body could even offer her that release. The thought of giving up finally demanded to be re-examined.

I'll die here. Do you hear me? I'll die before giving up my claim.

Telisa thought of Magnus and the others. She imagined telling them she had won. She *had* to win.

The agony continued. Her world became the ebb and flow of pain. Telisa slowly lost all context on her misery. She simply hurt. It went on and on.

At some point, she became aware that the light had disappeared. She floated in blackness. The pain was gone. She felt numb, traumatized.

Did I win or not?

The alien thought returned, resonating in her mind.

"The second trial is a trial of intelligence."

Telisa considered that in the void. Was she sharper than usual in this body? How did her mind think in different bodies?

My mind is no longer physically Terran, but surely even the Trilisk-brain-emulated version is still basically the same. The AIs must think I'm actually a Trilisk mind since I was pulled from a host body... are Terrans smarter than Trilisks? Is my mind dumber running on an alien architecture?

Telisa felt the answer was probably 'no'. The Trilisks had advanced to such levels they must have tinkered with their minds to expand their intellectual capacity. Terrans had begun that process with various genetic modifications, but they could not be on the level of the Trilisks.

A swatch of color caught her attention. In the blackness, she could not tell if the source was small or distant, but it grew into a swirling triangle that might be only a few meters away. Hundreds of tiny triangles resolved themselves within the main object, each glowing with its own hue.

The colorful triangles wriggled. Several of them rose from the plane of the main triangle. Others descended. Their colors wavered.

Telisa stared at the display. It could have been an alien map, a plan, or a work of art.

If I'm supposed to know what that is a priori, I'm going to fail the test.

The object pulsated and mutated before her steadily.

There's a pattern. There must be.

Telisa checked the color of the highest triangles. The peaks were either red or yellow, but there was one brown.

What if Trilisks have a broader range of vision that Terrans? What if there are colors here my mind can't even comprehend? I'll never win if I can't understand the input.

Telisa suppressed the panicked thought and concentrated on the wiggling grid. Though the triangles had bulged and warped into three-dimensional structures, they still remained more or less in an organized grid. As she looked at one, she became aware that she could adjust its height with a thought. She tried depressing one of the highest peaks. It slowly descended and changed color. The triangles in the vicinity changed color as well.

What would be the objective? To organize? Arrange? Flatten the board?

She played with more peaks, flattening them one at a time and observing the results.

Is there a conservation of height here? Of color? How does the height relate to the color? The movement?

There were many variables. She wondered if there were even more than she had noticed. She decided to try the color by itself first. The triangles of the same height were definitely not the same color.

So it's not a simple graphic relief map. The color is not indicative of the altitude.

Telisa kept playing with the peaks, searching for an intuitive understanding. She left the green triangles alone and tried to change the object to a uniform color. After several moves she noticed the colors had consolidated a bit, forming mostly greens and blues. Most of the reddish hues had gone.

I'll organize. Simplify. It's as good a choice as any.

When Telisa began filling in the trenches and valleys, her previous work fell apart. The colors diversified rapidly. She glanced around for a second to see if she was missing some other component. There was still nothing in the black void except herself and the colorful puzzle.

I guess I can have uniform shape, or maybe color, but not both. Or maybe that's the goal, but of course it's not easy.

Telisa decided to continue, searching for more clues. She kept making changes on instinct, looking for patterns. She felt she had to understand a few relationships before she could solve anything. Soon she had three colors vying for control of her triangle. A red patch dominated the top, and its average height came above the rest. On her left she saw a small green patch, then valleys descended on the right, mostly blue.

What if it's not supposed to be flat?

She now saw something uniform emerge from the original chaos—four smaller triangles within the larger one, with the upper triangle high and red, the left triangle level and green, and the right triangle deep and blue. The central inverted triangle that adjoined all the others was white and curved to join the others smoothly.

Telisa had no idea if the design was the objective, but she had no other leads, so she decided to see it through to perfection. She worked for what must have been ten or twenty more minutes. Her progress was slow, with a few regressions, but overall her display became better organized.

I almost have it—I hope.

She leveled the last incongruous components of the three sub-triangles with a few more moves.

There.

Telisa stood upon the flat planes of rock again. The heat had subsided. She did not see the other Trilisk with any of her three eyes.

A new communication popped into her mind.

"The third trial is a trial of intent. What do you seek to accomplish?"

Telisa did not answer immediately. She took a moment to consider her answer.

I hope these AIs were created by the ancient, wise Trilisks. I hope those Trilisks were not monstrous like the ones I've encountered. What if the race was once wise and peaceful? I could have a chance, right?

She tried to clear her mind, but new doubts arose.

Or am I just being a dumb Terran, hoping that the Trilisks were creatures I would find admirable?

Telisa wondered if she had all the time in the world to answer, or if her chance would time out.

It doesn't matter. I probably can't lie anyway.

Telisa decided to avoid deception. That left her trying to figure out what she really did want. It had said her intent. Was that short term or long term?

It probably means what is my current intent for the powers of the AI.

"I want to help the Celarans, protect them from extinction. I want to aid my own race as well, earn us our safety and freedom to live, explore, and learn more about the universe. In a nutshell, I want safety for us all, then knowledge."

Nothing happened for three seconds. Telisa was about to continue with more details when the other Trilisk winked back into being across from her.

"The trials are complete. We will now render our decision."

Telisa did not move. Her adversary also stood quiescent, awaiting the result.

"The candidates are of nearly equivalent worth. Support is withdrawn from both until separation, but each will retain one support module. This system will be spared further disturbance from conflicting directives."

"We will strive against you again," the other Trilisk told her. "When it is allowed."

All of that for what... a draw? How can you draw in three contests? I thought that was the point, but I guess each contest gave a score instead of a winner and loser.

The other Trilisk strode toward its recessed opening in the nearest cliffside. It tucked itself in perfectly, even pulling two of its legs into either edge of the front face until it became a part of the wall. From a distance, it might have even been mistaken for a cracked section of rock, if it were not for its cold squid-eye.

Then it utterly disappeared.

The creature's last message repeated in her mind.

'When it is allowed'. If the modules really are the AIs, then the devices that serve us also appear to have power, even over the Trilisks!

"Support module Jiggaurtraulix will now disable to prevent local catastrophe."

The thought came to Telisa's mind as a report, not a statement of the Trilisk.

The world popped out of existence, leaving Telisa without awareness of any reality at all.

Michael McCloskey

Chapter 27

Siobhan had many feeds of the installation in her PV. She concentrated on the section the PIT team occupied.

Stop the shaking. Protect us. Keep us safe. Block any dangerous energy beams that come toward us by cancelling out the EM waves perfectly.

Siobhan was so busy trying to use the AI she did not closely monitor her real vision. Some unconscious thread grabbed her attention. Caden concentrated next to her. She looked down the corridor. Telisa stood mere meters away. Her cloaking sphere had been disabled; she was plainly visible.

"She's back!" Siobhan declared.

"What happened?" Magnus demanded.

Telisa almost fell over. Magnus grabbed her arm and righted her. She took one ragged gasp. Siobhan was alarmed.

Telisa still looked stunned. Siobhan asked Telisa's suit for a diagnostic. It told Siobhan that everything was intact: Telisa had not been physically harmed, at least not that her suit was aware of.

What happened to her? What have they done? Used their AI to destroy her mind?

"We have to fight on our own. The AI won't work anymore," she croaked.

"What? Why?" asked Magnus.

"I met a Trilisk. It controls the Quarus, as we suspected."

"Met a Trilisk? *Where*?" Magnus asked.

"I have no idea. How long have I been gone?"

"Seconds," Magnus said.

"Only minutes," Caden answered at the same time. They looked at each other like idiots.

"It was less than a minute," Siobhan said.

"It doesn't matter. Whatever we have, muster it! Both AIs are useless. It's up to us now."

A hard determination arose in Siobhan that she had not felt since she went after the head of Spero.

She said it: It's up to us now.

"Only three assault machines left. Still plenty of attendants, though," Siobhan said.

"Use them offensively. Bludgeon the Quarus to death with them if you have to," Telisa said.

She's more bloodthirsty. Good. Unless it's because she's a real Trilisk now...

"I'll direct the assault machines in," Magnus said.

Siobhan received a pointer from Telisa showing an attack plan. The crossbar of the H-shaped station had two main corridors connecting the station's two sides. Siobhan and Caden were to assault along the northern corridor.

"Let's go!" Siobhan said. She hit Caden a glancing blow on the shoulder to accentuate her statement, then turned and ran for the corridor they had been assigned. After a moment, she saw him following after her as she flashed through attendant feeds.

Siobhan kept running. After two hundred meters, they reached the beginning of the cross corridor with Caden at her heels. She checked an attendant feed of the corridor. It looked clear, so she stepped out into it.

"Wait! Cover!" Caden said urgently.

Siobhan threw herself to the far side behind a support beam.

"Where?"

Caden brought up his rifle from a crouching position at the intersection. Bright light shone from farther down the corridor.

Destroyer.

A thump rattled through the structure she leaned against. Otherwise, no sound came from Caden's rifle, though it had launched a projectile.

"Kill," he confirmed, coming back to his feet. "It was just a drone, not a tank."

"What are we going to do if the next one IS a tank?" she asked, but she did not really expect an answer. If it did happen, they would have to shelter and wait for it to come into range of their breaker claws, then risk blowing themselves up with it.

They leapfrogged each other down the corridor, sprinting between spots that offered cover while the other watched from a sheltered firing position. Siobhan checked the tactical. There was only one Space Force assault robot left. Telisa, Magnus, and Arakaki were moving a bit slower down the southern station connector.

"Damage ahead," Caden pointed out.

Siobhan ran from cover and looked. The corridor's floor was cracked ahead. Siobhan barely slowed. A quick look through a transparent section of wall told her that they were about ten meters above the moon's surface here. If the foundations had shifted, it made sense that the base had to give somewhere, but she believed the bridge was still sound.

Siobhan hopped across the gap in the low gravity. The floor held. She reached her next cover point. There were no more Destroyers in sight. Caden took a position across from her.

"We're a third of the way," he said.

"The Quarus with their AI could be anywhere. It could be right ahead of us. Keep going!"

They resumed their leapfrog pattern down the corridor. Siobhan kept sharp, looking at every niche and through every window. The light gravity was wonderful. She was able to outdistance Caden easily with her long stride and ingrained low gravity hopping.

"More damage. This one looks worse," Caden said.

Siobhan emerged from cover and ran along beside him to get a view. The corridor ahead had been completely shattered. It resumed across a twenty-meter gap.

It's blown away. The Sharplight might have done that.

"Looks too dangerous. Maybe we should stop here," Caden said.

"We're not stopping. By the Five, Caden, don't you know me better than that by now?" Siobhan said. She increased speed instead of slowing down. The trench looked wide—too wide.

This is a small moon. Low gravity. I can make it.

Caden cursed. Siobhan did not check to see if he was coming after her. She knew he would.

She ran up to the edge and launched herself with everything she had. She hurled upward and forward, rising...

Siobhan's visor went black. Her suit immediately alerted her: overheating.

Siobhan reacted quickly. She had her attendants push her off course, hard. The beam, wherever it came from, must have stayed on her expected trajectory, because the heat warning slipped to a lower priority. Her suit was still too hot, but it was no longer getting hotter.

Siobhan landed hard on part of the support structure holding up the corridor. The moon was fifteen meters below her. Five meters above, the corridor resumed intact.

Caden dropped prone at the edge of the corridor on the other side.

"You're visible! Covering you. Jump back in there, if you can."

Siobhan glanced at her own arm, verifying that her cloaking was disabled. She looked up. Her way straight upward was blocked. She placed her feet against the piling she rested on and pushed upwards and to one side, looking for a better position to get back into the corridor.

Siobhan's link told her Caden's weapon had fired twice. She did not receive any hit reports. Since he had not said anything, she concentrated on getting into the corridor opening on the far side. After rebalancing herself, she pushed off toward it. She veered right, but an attendant nudged her back on course. She arrived with her upper half level with the floor. She struck, then anchored herself in place with her arms. Her Veer suit protected her from the ragged edge of the structure.

Siobhan's hold threatened to slip. She did not feel afraid to fall in the light gravity, but she did fear that her exposed lower body might be targeted at any moment. She heard a distant thump through the floor and looked up. Caden had jumped across. His ghostly form reached out to her, they joined hands, and he hauled her up into the corridor.

She smiled. They had made it to the other side. Siobhan breathed a bit easier.

"We have a tank headed toward us from outside the station," Caden warned. He passed a pointer to a video feed from a source outside the complex.

"Then we should—"

The wall beside them started to glow.

Fracksilvers.

***

Telisa leaped forward in the corridor, traveling ten meters to another alcove. Her attendant told her what was ahead: an armored door.

Magnus leveled his PAW at the door. He tried a round. Telisa watched the projectile fly toward the door. It moved quickly, but not so quickly her enhanced eyes and reflexes could not follow it. The round's jet continued to accelerate it after leaving the barrel. It struck but bounced off silently.

"Our armor piercing ammo isn't up to it," he summarized.

"Let's see how well they built this place," Telisa said. She took an ultrasharp blade off her hip and leaped to the ceiling. She grabbed a pipe and tested the blade.

The blade cut through the hull material smoothly. Telisa cut herself an escape hatch.

"Let's go over this hardpoint."

"Check the tactical first," Magnus said, but Telisa was already doing it. She did not see any Quarus war machines out there, but they had lost so many Terran machines and Vovokan attendants that their coverage was spotty.

Telisa slipped out anyway. Nothing fired at her.

The outer surface of the base was mostly smooth, though she saw a half dozen niches here and there within a few hundred meters. She hugged the top surface and crawled forward, making good time despite the awkwardness.

An attendant feed showed her that Magnus and Arakaki had followed suit. They all shuffled over the top of the base for thirty meters, hugging the surface.

"Back in here?"

Magnus nodded. "Hurry, we're too exposed."

Telisa cut into the building. The blade sliced through the material, but it was already giving more resistance.

The blade is ruined. That's fine, as long as it gets us back in here...

Telisa cut three sides of a square, making a flap, then pried it open, exercising her immense strength. An attendant darted in and gave the all clear. She slid smoothly inside after it.

Telisa checked for enemies. She had cut into a long room, at least twenty meters wide and forty meters long. She stood next to a bay in a section of recessed floor. Open-ended, flexible tubes pointed up and outward like a huge flower. Four metal mounts came up from the center.

Are those for their crab-legs? A Quarus works here?

She saw more bays and five pieces of rectangular equipment with smoothed corners, three meters on a side. The walls were mostly white but held glossy black panels every few meters. More tubes descended from the ceiling in three places.

Are those data connections? Oxygen supply? Water pumps? Ah. Maybe this room can fill with water when there's a crew working here?

Back the way they had come, she saw the other side of the armored door and a small room she imagined was a security point. The ceiling just past the door was obscured.

Might be a laser mount in there. Best to stay back and figure out what this place is.

"This place looks different. It's not the connector corridor, and not a factory floor, either," Arakaki said as she dropped down from their new entrance.

A monstrous machine emerged into the corridor thirty meters ahead. It looked like a metallic Quarus, with four long support legs supporting a tank-like body the size of a single-person land taxi. A weapons turret hung from the underside.

The team dove for cover. Telisa found a spot behind one of the rectangular objects.

"What *is* that thing?" Telisa asked.

"I don't know, but it's ugly," Arakaki said.

"Let's hope it can't detect us," Magnus said.

A special war machine could mean that we're close to something important... the AI.

Magnus traded looks with Telisa. Even cloaked, looking only at his virtual location outline, she could tell he was thinking the same thing.

The machine fired at Arakaki's position in one of the bays. Telisa could tell some of the energy was coming through into her recessed cover.

"Argggh!" Arakaki grunted angrily.

Even in pain, she growls instead of howls. Tough as nails.

Telisa ran up a side wall and launched herself straight across the room in front of the machine. The energy weapon left Arakaki's spot and tracked Telisa for a moment, causing her suit to give an alarm. Her suit heated up. Then, as Telisa shot across the corridor, the turret had to stop because one of the machine's crablike legs blocked its line of sight.

Telisa activated her breaker claw before it could resume cooking her.

The explosion could almost be missed in the vacuum. Telisa's unnaturally sharp eyes caught a glimpse of shrapnel flying from its underside. Sharp impacts pounded against her right side. The machine hopped up in silence, then settled slowly in the low gravity, frozen. It hit the ground and lay still.

"Got it!" she announced.

Her Veer suit reported mildly reduced integrity.

The machine clambered back up. The energy emitter turret on its underside had been blown away, leaving an apron of jagged metal around a hole.

"It's still working! I've never seen that before," she said.

"Telisa! You're visible!" Magnus warned.

The machine leaped to attack. The ends of its legs opened into pincers. As it flew toward her, two of the legs reached forward to grab her.

Her now-dull sword clanged off one pincer without doing damage, but it knocked the leg aside, preventing the robot's appendage from slicing her in half.

The other pincer darted in from her right. Telisa jumped over it with amazing speed, spun in midair, and pushed off the ceiling to evade the strike.

Magnus appeared in the open. He was also now fully visible. He charged the machine.

"Stay back!" Telisa warned, but he was already committed. He fired at least ten rounds from his space-operations PAW, but they bounced off the machine harmlessly. One of the ricochets stung Telisa's thigh through the Veer suit, and another hit her foot. One of the pincers shot out to intercept Magnus.

No!

At the last moment, Magnus's attendants thrust his upper body down and back, evading the pincer. His momentum slid him under the machine. Telisa blocked a pincer with her arm, putting all her strength into it. She could not push it away, but instead, sent herself flying to one side in the low gravity.

Arakaki focused a laser on a bulb on the upper half of the machine, presumably trying to blind it or burn through a sensor mount. Magnus emptied his clip into the bottom of the machine where the turret had been blown off.

That should kill it! No armor left down there.

The machine halted. Telisa flew ten meters beyond it and got a look at Magnus. He looked intact.

Magnus mechanically reloaded his PAW and shot four more rounds into the robot, taking the time to direct them into four separate spots.

"I really think it's dead this time," Arakaki gasped.

Arakaki's suit told Telisa's link that it was still critically overheated. Telisa's own Veer suit had absorbed half as much heat as it could withstand. The ricochet impact spots were minor. The suit told her the impacts had only compromised it by ten percent overall, to add to the previous five percent done by the shrapnel.

"I don't know what that thing did, but our cloaking is fragged," Arakaki said. They could see each other plainly.

Telisa checked the tactical.

"We may have lost the AI backup, but we still have the *Sharplight*," Magnus reminded her. "Might as well use the fire support."

"I've lost contact with Siobhan and Caden," Telisa said.

"We would risk hitting their AI," Arakaki pointed out.

"I think the AIs will make it. It would stand to reason that they can protect themselves," Telisa said.

Yes, but they're disabled. Is it as durable as other Trilisk constructs? Probably...

"Barrai. Open fire on the far side of the base," ordered Telisa. She sent a pointer with the zone she wanted to hit. Based on where Siobhan and Caden were when they left the tactical, she judged they could not have made it into the fire zone, if they were still alive.

"Aye aye, TM," Lieutenant Barrai said. Her voice sounded shell-shocked.

If she's been watching this, I'm surprised she responded at all.

The area shook yet again. Explosions blossomed over the tactical, unheard by the team in the eerie vacuum.

"I have attendant feeds and more targets," Barrai said.

Telisa received a message on her channel from ACBM Mamba.

"Twelve targets identified and neutralized."

The targets came up on the tactical. The map showed vast devastation visited upon the base, clustered with so many items of interest Telisa had to start filtering them out.

The deactivation of the AI must have caused that interference to drop. Their protection is gone.

"Seventeen more targets identified and neutralized."

The Mamba provided pointers with even more information. Telisa accessed a map of the dozen Quarus and seventeen Destroyers that had been killed.

"It could be at one of these spots," Telisa said. "Get the attendants over to them. I have this one. Magnus, you take that one."

The base rocked again.

A priority message came in. It was a map pointer.

"Another explosion. A big one!" Magnus said.

"There was another Quarus there," Marcant said. "The Mamba neutralized it."

"Damn," Magnus said. "Maybe they destroyed the AI rather than let it fall into our hands."

"It could be a trick," Arakaki said.

"This is probably a weapons factory," Telisa said. "There are bound to be some impressive explosions given this kind of damage. Keep looking for that signature. Maybe we'll find it somewhere else."

They continued to search, but Telisa had a feeling they would never find it.

Michael McCloskey

Chapter 28

Telisa was happy for one second when she awakened until she remembered the price they had paid for victory. She rolled over in her sleep web, alone in her quarters.

Caden and Siobhan. Gone.

It had taken them a while to reconstruct what had happened in all the chaos, but the attendant feeds eventually made it clear. As the *Sharplight* had carved up the far side of the platform, the PIT team had charged ahead to attack, led by groups of surviving attendants and backed by the ACBM Mamba. Then a large Quarus combat machine opened fire on Caden and Siobhan's side of the platform.

Telisa squeezed her eyes shut against the tears. All the old regrets came back.

We're supposed to be explorers, not soldiers.

She took a deep breath.

It's almost over. Just have to clean up. Then we can go... where? Back to Shiny?

The Space Force and PIT team had collected a lot of Quarus technology they could share with the Vovokan who ruled Sol. Telisa felt only anger thinking about Shiny. She did not want to go back. The alien's attempted manipulation of Siobhan highlighted how bad their master was—they *could not* go back.

Telisa checked the fleet disposition. Most of the manned ships were out beyond the remains of the asteroids and ready to ramp up their gravity spinners to levels necessary for interstellar travel. Robotic elements were still carefully backing away, taking every precaution they could. No one believed the Quarus had much left in them, but of course, caution ruled the day.

It was time to leave the system. What did they call it in the Space Force?

Strategic redeployment.

She opened a channel to Admiral Sager. He connected quickly.

"What happened back there, exactly?" Sager asked.

"The team came through for us," Telisa said. "We neutralized their superweapon, though we lost two TMs in the action. Siobhan and Caden are gone." Her voice was flat and hollow.

"I'm sad to hear it," Sager replied. "The Quarus defense network has crumbled. We await your orders."

"Now, we'll deliver our ultimatum and leave. QC2 and QC3 stay intact," Telisa commanded.

Sager tactfully waited for a moment, then spoke.

"After our losses, just leaving might be hard for some in the Space Force to swallow," Sager said. "We could set up an occupation force here."

"I think we've eliminated the Trilisks," Telisa said. "What will happen here will be very similar to Sol after our revolution. We'll leave Aiye's sensor network though, at least for now, so we can keep eyes on them."

That seemed to satisfy Sager. If the Quarus retained their xenophobic crusade in the absence of the Trilisk influence, at least the Space Force would get an early warning of it. And if Trilisks returned, then someone would come to eradicate them again.

Telisa broke the connection and opened a new channel to Lee.

"Lee, is the story ready to transmit to the Quarus?"

"It's a ripe vine ready to drain," Lee affirmed. "As you know, Quarus communications are as long as a hundred-cycle-old vine. The story includes how Terrans have entered into a mutual defense pact with Celarans, which includes a full exchange of all technologies. Our vines are intertwined now, and we share the same sap. All this is clear in the message."

"I read it as best I could," Marcant said. "The Celarans have done a great job with it. Of course, we don't really know how weird it sounds to a Quarus."

"As long as they understand it."

"I feel confident they will," he said.

"Send it please," Telisa told Lee. "Let's hope we never come back here."

Telisa considered wandering back to her quarters, or seeking out Magnus. Her voracious appetite had been suppressed by her mood, but she knew it would return. Her Trilisk-designed body needed a lot of calories.

She took two steps toward the mess when Adair contacted her.

"Achaius is coming for the AI. It will kill for it. Recommend giving it up and saving yourselves."

Telisa accepted Adair's message without question. She did not waste time wondering at the sudden appearance of the missing AIs, which had been presumed lost. The threat kickstarted her mind into a flurry.

The AI is in the vault, but the Trilisk robot no longer protects it... what can stop a Vovokan battle sphere? Our breaker claws?

Telisa wanted to ask questions, but Adair's communication had been one way, without a full connection. That intimated that Adair was in a bad way. Perhaps it had fought with Achaius and lost?

She opened a channel to Barrai but let Magnus and Arakaki listen in. The others might not connect in time to hear it live, but they would be able to listen to the conversation from their link logs whenever they responded.

"Barrai, seal up the ship. No one in or out. Warn off any shuttles. No one to dock. If anything approaches, open fire on it. Remove Achaius from any security protocols you own and dial security up to the tightest level. I'll handle the rest. This is not a drill."

"What's up?" Magnus responded rapidly but calmly.

Telisa removed Achaius from the PIT channel and replied on it.

"Achaius is going for the AI. I don't know why, but it's dangerous now. Possibly it's under alien control, but all that matters is we have to stop it by any means."

It only took Magnus a second to absorb the news.

"Telisa, none of us are a match for that battle sphere."

"We can't let it take the AI. Whatever it wants, if it's going to seize the artifact by force then it can't be good."

Best case scenario, Achaius only wants to take the AI and start a civilization of its own somewhere far from here. But that still leaves us without our best tool.

"Barrai, Marcant, Maxsym. Stay where you are. Fire on Achaius on sight."

"What makes you believe he's betrayed us?" Marcant said.

Can't blame him for defending his friend. This should defuse it.

"Adair is the one who told me," Telisa said. Marcant did not reply.

"I'll try and move the AI before Achaius gets here," Telisa said. "If we can't fight it, start brainstorming. We need serious firepower."

"We could set off the armory when it gets there and blow it to hell," Arakaki said.

"Pray for it to be hidden in place?" Maxsym suggested. "We could make it invisible and Achaius would think it's been moved."

"If the AI comes back online, do it," Telisa said. "I'll move it when I get there."

She had been moving so quickly, she was already only thirty seconds away from the vault.

Telisa was about to tell Arakaki to rig the armory when a message came through.

"We have a hull breach!" Barrai reported.

Telisa found it on the map. It was exactly where someone would breach the ship to head through a cargo bay toward the bridge... and its armory where the AI rested.

"Arakaki, good idea but no time. It's headed there already."

"Telisa, don't get trapped there!" Magnus urged.

Telisa sprinted on. Her mind raced as well.

I'm in a super-fast, super-strong body. How can I stop that thing?

The first answer was to pray to the AI, but it was still disabled, and that was a *good* thing, because otherwise Achaius would be able to use it as well.

She reached the vault. The AI sat inside, dark. It no longer scintillated in its mysterious way. Telisa grabbed it and ran out.

As one of Telisa's feet pushed off, she felt vibration in the deck.

That thing is coming straight for me.

Telisa sprinted through the bridge and down an adjacent corridor, heading away from the breach point. She thought as furiously as she ran.

Telisa connected to Sager at the highest priority.

"Admiral Sager, we have a grave situation. Cordon the *Sharplight*. If any spacecraft leave this ship, take them out."

"Aye, TM," the response came. It sounded sleepy, but firm.

Poor man probably thought he could finally sleep after the battle.

She dashed through an open blast door between sections of the ship.

Where can I go that it can't fit?

Telisa took a sharp right down a maintenance corridor meant for robots. On her right, a vertical access tube lay open, allowing for movement between decks. It was narrow.

Telisa hopped into the tube and climbed upwards.

"What's wrong? Should we send help?" Sager asked.

"Send in your best assault unit. Or the Avatar! We have a rogue battle sphere and it wants our toys!"

It will be too late.

"I'm setting up an ambush," Magnus sent her. The message came with a map pointer. He was toward the aft of the *Sharplight*. Telisa was headed in the wrong direction.

She passed a blast bulkhead and ordered it to close. As she ran, she felt a wave of heat behind her.

Ka-Boom!

She did not have to look. The sphere was close, and it was not letting doors get in its way. It had the power to blast through anything except maybe the ship's battle shields.

So much for that. It'll just damage the ship more. But maybe it drains some of its reserves...

"Head back aft once you near the bulkhead," Magnus sent her again. "I'm setting up in this shuttle bay. Maybe our shuttle weapons can hurt it."

"I can't lead it to you. It'll vaporize you."

"You have a better plan? That thing is stronger than any Terran assault machine," Marcant said.

That thing is run by your friend.

Fooosh! WHAP!

Telisa's heightened senses felt a pressure change. A bright light flashed. Then something as hard as ceramic plating hit her across her entire back. She flew forward out of control.

The AI broke from her grasp. Telisa exhaled as her body absorbed the shock wave. She grunted like a prize fighter taking a liver kick.

Her host body recovered in a fraction of a second. She cleared her head and found her footing. The AI was only meters away. She darted toward it.

A flash of heat warned her away. An energy beam had been placed between her and the AI.

No!!!

Telisa had to turn and run. If she went for the AI, she would die, and there would be no future for her. She fled.

"Achaius has the AI! It's getting away!" Telisa yelled, transmitted the message with the same urgency.

"I can't stop it," Magnus said. "Maybe the Space Force can."

Telisa dove down a tube, headed for a lower level.

Crack! BOOOOM!

The ship shook like an almost empty can of nuts in a giant's grasp, and Telisa was a nut. She fell to the next level, then flopped back up to hit the ceiling, then the deck again.

Alerts rolled into her link. The *Sharplight* had taken massive damage.

I told Sager to shoot on escaping ships, not us! Has he taken matters into his own hands?

"Who's shooting at us?" Magnus demanded.

"This is Barrai. I've taken Achaius out with ship's weapons."

"What? The *Sharplight* can—"

"Fire upon itself? Yes, if you know which nine safety measures to disable. Which I learned how to do when I took this assignment. My superior told me to prepare this contingency when I came on to serve the PIT team."

Should I be thankful or afraid?

Telisa trusted Barrai in her gut. Then she thought about Achaius. She had not seen any warning signs of its imminent betrayal.

"Good work, Lieutenant," she croaked. She felt certain she had only lived because of her special physiology.

"Not to be callous, but is the AI destroyed?" Arakaki interjected.

"Let's go find out."

Chapter 29

Magnus waited with Telisa on the bridge for a meeting with Admiral Sager. He kept an eye on the fleet withdrawal in his PV. The entire fleet had reached the outer system and prepared to depart for good.

Telisa opened a channel for them and added Sager. He connected within five seconds.

"I trust the withdrawal is proceeding without any snags," Telisa said.

"It is, TM."

"Good. Do you have any questions?"

"Is the AI intact?"

"It is," Telisa said. "At least as far as I can tell. It hasn't turned back on yet, though, and I don't expect it will until we've left this system."

"Are there any other missions on the horizon we should be aware of?" Sager asked.

Telisa was silent for a long moment.

"I've been thinking about using our alien technology to liberate Sol," Telisa admitted.

Sager frowned.

She's putting him in a difficult position. He behaves as though he likes her more than Shiny, but is that an act?

"If I may, TM," Sager began. Telisa nodded.

"Earth doesn't want a visionary leader to free them from Shiny and show them the way into the future. Earth wants guard dogs."

"How so?"

"All that Core Worlders care about is their virtual activities; the real world is just an annoying distraction for most of them. As long as they can do what they want, play with who they want, they don't care about what goes on in reality. They love Shiny because he leaves them to it. He doesn't try to rule them, restrict them, or interfere with them in any way that they care about. For a while there, they woke up and panicked about the hostile aliens. But now that they believe the Space Force and Shiny are going to keep them safe, they're back to their games."

"So you're saying Sol doesn't need saving."

Sager nodded. "Pretty much, yes."

"What should we do, then?"

"Well, I believe in guarding Terrans, even if they barely know I exist. You love to explore and learn about the universe, yes? Especially aliens? Then that's what you should do. Go and explore."

Telisa smiled. "You're acting very fatherly today."

"Then let me say your father would be proud of you."

"Good luck, Admiral." Telisa closed the connection.

"He's right," Magnus said.

"Thank you."

Telisa made no move to leave. She looked thoughtful.

"So if we pass on trying to wrest Sol from Shiny—and I agree with Sager that maybe it's not worth attempting—what would we do?" he asked her.

"The Cylerans were very happy to discover that the space station we visited is still intact, even if infested with Blackvines. They're going to recolonize it."

"It should help them recover, though it's a lot less than a whole planet. What would we do, though? Help them with the Blackvines?"

"I want to call the other teams to join us there. That should give us a huge boost in creating a sanctuary from which we could work to oppose Shiny, or at least, stand independent of him."

"If you call them, then Shiny will learn of it," Magnus warned. "He'll come and shut us down. Maybe for good."

Telisa paused. Magnus saw Marcant show up on the channel.

"Marcant, can we send messages to our duplicate team members without Shiny finding out?"

"If it were only other Terrans we were up against, definitely. But Shiny..."

Marcant did not continue for a moment. Telisa assumed he was conferring with Adair. The Terran AI had returned to the ship in an attendant. The PIT team had hailed Adair as a hero.

"It's too risky," he concluded. "If I *had* to do it, I wouldn't send anything to Sol. We could send the message out on the frontier and catch the other teams there. Still, Shiny is always collecting everything he wants from the Terran network. I think he'd figure it out. And even if he didn't, surely he's listening in on some of the teams? Would they slip up and give it away?"

Telisa nodded.

"We'll think on it further," Magnus said. "Maybe we can't move on it until we have a better plan."

"While we're speaking of pie in the sky projects, there's another objective we need to put some effort into," Telisa said.

"What?"

"We have a Trilisk column on the *Iridar*, and a Trilisk AI. Shiny's way ahead of us here, but if we can get these things working, then it's possible we could get our people back. Siobhan, Caden, Cilreth, and Imanol."

"You mean we could get *some* Cilreth and *some* Imanol. Not ours, exactly," Magnus said.

"I'll take it. They were both great TMs... Listen to me, now I'm using that title like Sager and Barrai."

"Would Jason be in there?"

"He might be. I don't know. Imagine if we could get any of them back. Wouldn't it be amazing?"

Magnus had a negative gut reaction as he first thought about it. Was making people out of thin air, even people they knew, a good idea? However, when he tried to consider it rationally, he decided it made sense.

"Yeah, I'd like to have them back. I assume they would *want* to be brought back..."

Arakaki is the only one of us that I think has actually looked forward to death from time to time.

"Then we work toward it. We can look forward to achieving it someday."

Someday, indeed.

***

Magnus asked the ship for Telisa's location. She was in his quarters. Usually, they met in her quarters unless he happened to already be in his when she sought him out.

That's strange.

He strode to his room, curiosity piqued. Telisa stood inside, waiting for him.

"Happy birthday!" Telisa exclaimed. "At least, by ship's clock. Who knows how far off Earth time we are by now?"

She referred to the time they had spent at significant fractions of the speed of light, usually in combat situations around star systems. Luckily, their gravity spinners did not introduce large time skews when allowing them to break the light barrier, as the physics of that mode of travel were completely different and utterly confusing.

"Thank you... did you get me something?"

"I did. Come here."

Telisa sat at a table she had folded out of the wall. She set her elbow on the surface and held her hand up. She motioned for him to clasp it.

They had done this test several times before. Magnus had no hope of defeating her in arm wrestling since she had taken her host body—Telisa was at least four times stronger now. Magnus decided to let her play her little game, whatever it was.

He sat across from her and gripped her hand.

"Ready? Go!" Telisa said.

Magnus braced himself for a good arm-wrenching. But this time, her arm did not assail his like a hydraulic press. Magnus adapted and put all his strength into it. Her arm collapsed and Telisa flopped with it.

"Ugh. You win," she said.

He smiled.

"My birthday present is that you let me win an arm wrestling match?" he asked.

"I didn't let you win. That's as strong as I am right now."

Magnus's eyebrows rose.

"What happened? How are you in your own body?"

"I'm not. This is still the host body, but Maxsym gave me a paralytic nerve agent. One of his failed attempts to find a poison for the Trilisks."

"He *poisoned* you? This is the most confusing birthday I can recall."

Telisa looked down at the table. Her fingertip moved lightly across the surface.

"I thought you might... well, I thought both of us might enjoy it if... we spent a night the way it used to be. You know, before I moved into a Trilisk host body..."

Magnus blinked. He had never complained about her increased strength—except perhaps in jokes—but she had perceived that it subtly changed their dynamic in bed.

"I could get on board for that," he said. "As long as it's just one night. We need Trilisk Special Forces back tomorrow."

She nodded. "Just one night..."

Michael McCloskey

Chapter 30

A massive Vovokan battleship arrived on station above a beautiful blue planet.

The tatters of the Quarus defense network had not even detected the cloaked leviathan that had encroached. Even if it had, it was no match for the invader.

Kirizzo3 lay curled within a complex control module deep in the belly of the ship. Information from the ships' countless sensors marched into his long spinal brain, showing that the Quarus had emerged from their underwater bunkers and fortresses to begin the process of rebuilding.

Kirizzo3 considered abandoning his master's directives and concentrating his efforts on escape. He decided the risk was too great.

The directive is reasonable. This threat must be eliminated.

He commanded the battleship to open fire.

THE END of The Celaran Pact (continued in The Rovan Ruins)

From the Author

Thanks for reading! As an indie author, I rely on your ratings and reviews to legitimize my work to those who have not read me. Please review this book on Amazon or Goodreads. Thank you.

Made in the USA
Coppell, TX
19 May 2023

17041457R00134